Annie B.,
MADE FOR TV

Annie B., MADE FOR TV

AMY DIXON

RP|KIDS
PHILADELPHIA

Running Press Kids
Hachette Book Group
1290 Avenue of the Americas, New York, NY 10104
www.runningpress.com/rpkids
@RP_Kids

Printed in the United States of America

First Edition: June 2018

Published by Running Press Kids, an imprint of Perseus Books, LLC, a subsidiary of Hachette Book Group, Inc. The Running Press Kids name and logo is a trademark of the Hachette Book Group.

The Hachette Speakers Bureau provides a wide range of authors for speaking events. To find out more, go to www.hachettespeakersbureau.com or call (866) 376-6591.

The publisher is not responsible for websites (or their content) that are not owned by the publisher.

Print book cover and interior design by T. L. Bonaddio

Library of Congress Control Number: 2017959793

ISBNs: 978-0-7624-6385-5 (hardcover),
978-0-7624-6384-8 (ebook)

LSC-C

10 9 8 7 6 5 4 3 2 1

FOR MOM AND DAD,
MY FIRST AND FOREVER
TROUBADOURS.

CHAPTER 1

"Jefferson, Jefferson, Home of the Quail!

Jefferson, Jefferson, we never fail!

Our school is the best, better than the rest.

We'll shout it loud and clear,

Jefferson, Jefferson, Home of the Quail,

Show us how you CHEER!"

I know as a fifth grader I'm supposed to roll my eyes and *pretend* to say the words to our school fight song instead of actually saying them. It's the little kids that get excited and belt out the lyrics and cheer their heads off at the end. The fifth graders, the rulers of the school, are supposed to cross their arms over their chest and act bored. Usually I play along, but today is our last day at Jefferson Elementary, and I can't help but sing and scream like a maniac at the end. I've been at this school since I was four years old, which means I've probably sung the phrase "Jefferson, Jefferson, Home of the Quail" seven thousand times.

Quail are the worst mascots ever. The quail is our state bird in California, so I'm pretty sure that's why it's our school mascot. I once did a report on quail and discovered they get scared easily and run away and hide when anyone comes close to them. So I'm not sure why you would want your school to be represented by a bird like that. If you're going to be a bird, at least pick a strong and brave bird, like an eagle or a hawk. When you play another school in basketball, you don't want to be the bird that gets eaten. You want to be the bird that eats the other birds!

The only mascot that's possibly worse is a troubadour. That was my mom's school mascot when she was my age. The first problem with a troubadour is that they don't even exist anymore. They're from way back in the time of knights and castles and damsels in distress. The second problem is that a troubadour is a wandering minstrel—someone who frolics around the countryside playing music and spouting love poetry. I'll never understand who thought that would make a good mascot. A mascot should be something you're scared to compete against. Troubadours just stand on the sidelines in their tights and funky hats, singing and waving to the real warriors. They're like the cheerleaders of the Middle Ages. What's scary about that? Oh, mighty troubadour, with your flute and tiny guitar, your inspiring poetry has me shaking in my boots! How will I handle all of your encouragement? The only chance you have with that one is to hope that no one knows what a troubadour is. Then you can pretend it's something fierce, like a rare type of jungle cat or a ferocious dinosaur species. But there's no pretending with a quail. Everyone knows what a quail is, and no one is afraid of it.

My best friend, Savannah, doesn't agree. She adores quail and was super upset when she saw them on the menu at Chez Jacques, a fancy-pants restaurant downtown. Which really just proves my point, since you would never see sautéed eagle or poached hawk on someone's dinner plate. But Savannah thinks quail are beautiful. Personally, I think they look a bit like a miniature soccer ball. Something you'd like to kick, which, again, makes them not the greatest mascot. But today, on the last day of fifth grade at "Jefferson, Jefferson, Home of the Quail," every student in the room wants to have the heart of a quail.

The Heart of a Quail Award is the biggest and best award you can get at our school. It is given to one fifth grader each year who represents

"Outstanding scholarship, active participation, dedicated school service, and positive leadership." The teachers like to call it the "school spirit" award, but I call it the "I'm good at everything" award. And even though I'm hardly ever the best at anything, there's a tiny part of me that thinks there's a chance my name could be called up to that stage. So my entire class is sitting here, actually holding it together pretty well for the last day of school, waiting for the awards to be announced. It's first thing in the morning, which helps because we haven't been here long enough to get antsy yet. We're sitting on the floor of the MPR, and it's super gross. The school calls it the multipurpose room because they use it for everything. It's the auditorium, but it's also the cafeteria and the gym, which means that this floor has been splattered on a regular basis with both taco sauce and wrestling sweat. Somehow, even when it's a hundred degrees outside, they manage to make the MPR absolutely freezing. Which feels great when you first walk in, but after thirty seconds it feels like you're inside an igloo. Thank goodness today I remembered my soccer hoodie. Now if they could only get it to smell like something other than dirty socks and tater tots in here, it might be bearable. Wait! That gives me a really good idea.

Kids, tired of sipping warm juice boxes in a cafeteria that smells like your worst nightmare? Ready to give your nose a break from today's lunch surprise?

INTRODUCING THE

smell SMASHER

the air freshener you wear like a fashion accessory! Earrings that smell like root beer? We've got 'em. Pins that give off the scent of your favorite bubble gum? Right here. Our necklaces are not only shaped like roses; they smell like roses, too! Look no further—THE SMELL SMASHER gets rid of those pesky smells and makes you look smashing in the process!

I love writing commercials. It's a talent that I discovered a few years ago when I used to watch cartoons. The cartoons were okay, but the made-for-TV commercials were so much more interesting. Pillow Pal—is it a pillow or a stuffed animal? Brilliant! Moon Munch—do you play with it or eat it? So creative! It was then that I realized writing was my passion in life. My dad's a writer, too, so I get my writing gene from him. Except I mostly like to write about my inventions, so Dad calls me a *wrinventor*. A writer-inventor.

A familiar voice calls out from the side of the auditorium. "Annie!"

I turn and see my mom and dad leaning forward out of their folding chairs. Dad has both hands in the air, giving me a giant double thumbs-up. "Go get 'em, honeykin!" I wish he wouldn't call me that at school. *Honeykin* is some mishmash of nicknames he has for me. First it was *honeypie*, followed by *pumpkin*, which now has become *honeykin*. Making up words is Dad's specialty. He said things like *fantabulous* and *ginormous* for years before they became actual words other people used. So he is a wrinventor, too. A wrinventor of words.

My teacher, Mr. Lombardi, is on the microphone now, which means it's time for awards. "Welcome, everyone, to our end-of-the-year awards ceremony!" A screech echoes through the auditorium, and some of the parents cover their ears. The sound system in here is terrible, so us kids are used to the piercing noise the mic makes. It doesn't help that Mr. Lombardi is super loud. I never really understood what it meant to have a "booming" voice until I was in his class. He booms way more than he talks. At first I was kind of scared of him, but then I discovered how goofy he really is. He likes to wear costumes when we study historical figures, and some days, to mix it up, he wears funny hats. It's pretty impossible to be afraid of someone in a hat.

Today, because it's a special day, he has on a black fedora with a red feather sticking out of it. "Thanks especially to all the parents who have taken the time to come out and support your children. We couldn't do it without you!" Then he calls out the names of the kids who made the honor roll, followed by sports awards, and then special academic awards. Savannah, who is sitting right next to me, has straight As, is the track team MVP, and wins a plaque for reading the most words in the entire school. She keeps having to get up and then squeeze back into her tiny space between me and Jake Ramirez. Meanwhile, I'm getting a cramp in my leg from sitting cross-legged on the floor for so long.

Finally, my name is called and I go up front to get a certificate for reaching my reading goal. Mom and Dad are super loud as I walk up, and all grins and flailing arms when I walk back to my spot on the floor. As I sit down, Savannah grabs my hand. "Heart of a Quail is up next!" she squeals. I turn to face her and squeal along, when I see that somehow, between getting up for MVP and Reading Champ, she managed to get a huge smear of ketchup on the front of her white ruffled shirt.

"What happened?" I ask, pointing to the giant red blob on her chest.

Mr. Lombardi is back on the mic. "And now, the moment you've all been waiting for. . . ."

Savannah's eyes follow my finger down to the ketchup, and get wide. She looks at her hand, which also has ketchup on it, and traces it down to a spot on the floor where, clearly, someone went condiment crazy at breakfast.

". . . It's time for the very special Heart of a Quail Award."

Savannah is rubbing frantically at the red on her shirt, trying to make it go away, but it's only making the spot bigger. It used to be a tiny puddle, but now it's a lake.

I'm trying to focus on Mr. Lombardi, because this is the moment. I know it's a long shot, but until he says something different, there's still a chance the name "Annie Brown" might come out of his mouth.

"This year's Heart of a Quail Award recipient is . . ."

Mr. Lombardi is trying to be dramatic, and drags out the "is" for way too long. The little kids are into it, and they start pounding the ground, creating a drumroll effect. I'm holding my breath, and wishing he would just say the name already. Finally, the drumroll dies down, and Mr. Lombardi booms once again into the microphone. "Savannah Summerlyn!"

Savannah stays seated, and for a second I can't figure out why she isn't popping up like she did for all the other awards. She's holding a hand over her heart like she's about to pledge her allegiance. I'm clapping and nudging her, not sure why she isn't moving, until I see the red peeking out from between her fingers. Oh, right. I quickly unzip my hoodie and hold it out to her. She doesn't seem to understand at first, so I help her put one arm through and something finally clicks into place. She zips it up over the mess and hugs me before she moves toward the stage. "You're the best, Annie!"

The words play in my head as I watch her skip up the stage steps. I certainly don't feel like the best when it comes to grades or sports or anything else that seems to matter at this school.

Savannah's pop is back, and before taking the award from Mr. Lombardi, she dips down into a dramatic curtsy. Everyone laughs and claps even louder. Savannah wins. I hardly have time to feel proud or disappointed, because Savannah is back with her arm around me, and our parents are taking pictures. Savannah can't even hold up all of her awards. She has to rest the Heart of a Quail Award, a heavy glass trophy in the shape of a bird, in the fold of her elbow. I hold up my single reading certificate and say, "Cheese!"

"Wait!" Mr. Lombardi says, running over and pulling the certificate out of my hand. "It's covering up the quail," he explains. "That's better," he says, moving the paper to my other hand. "I need to get a quick shot for our website. Annie, can you scooch a little that way?" I move a step farther away from Savannah and hear the click of the camera.

"Perfect!" Mr. Lombardi says, showing us the picture on the back of his camera. Savannah's right in the middle, smiling big and proud. But I was moving when he took it, so you can't even tell it's me. I'm just a blur near the edge. I think Mr. Lombardi sees me looking funny at it, because he says, "We can fix it up once we get it on the computer. A little of this, a little of that, a crop here and there. . . . It'll be great! We wouldn't want a picture of Savannah without her sidekick!"

Everyone keeps coming over to congratulate Savannah, which forces me to keep moving farther away to make room for them. Finally, Mom and Dad ask if they can walk me back to class, and I'm tired of waiting, so I agree. I give Savannah a little wave as we leave the MPR. She's chatting with people and passing around her award, so she doesn't see me.

My parents gush over my reading certificate as we walk to my classroom, where I'll waste away the rest of the last day of school. They tell me they're proud of me, but I can't help but wonder what it is exactly that they're proud of. Because as far as I can tell, the only thing I'm best at is being the friend of someone who is always the best at everything. Savannah's sidekick. There to clap for her and cover up her ketchup stains. A blur at the edge of the photo. And as I hug my parents good-bye and head back into my fifth-grade classroom for one last afternoon, I'm thinking it might be time to brush up on my poetry skills. Because I may not have the heart of a quail, but I'm shaping up to be a fabulous troubadour.

CHAPTER 2

The last day of school is supposed to be the best one. That's the rule. And it's especially the rule when it's your last day of all of elementary school. We've been in fifth grade now for nine months, which in kid time is longer than forever. Nine months of changing out of my soccer-ball pajama bottoms because they're not "presentable." Nine months of desperately smoothing the crinkles out of my homework in time to hand it in. Nine months of trying to perfect the face that says to my teacher, "I've never been more fascinated," when really I'm writing a made-for-TV commercial for my latest invention. I'm rocking that face right now, because I have the best idea.

Kids, tired of having to answer the dreaded question, "How was school today?" Wish you could tell your parents and friends how you're feeling, but can't find the words? Well, sing the blues no more. . . .

INTRODUCING THE

FEELINGS FOLDER

One glance at THE FEELINGS FOLDER and all will be revealed. Give a hug to someone whose folder is Bummed-out Blue. Jump on a trampoline with the person whose folder is Happy Sunshiny Yellow. And if you see red, run for your life!

Every student should be required to have a Feelings Folder. That way you would know who to ask for help when you don't understand an assignment, or who you definitely don't want to sit next to after we've had baked beans for lunch. Since today is the last day of school, I'm pretty sure most kids' folders would be bright yellow. Savannah's would be yellow for sure. I'm still deciding what color mine would be. Probably some splotchy rainbow mix, since my feelings are a big tangled-up mess.

"Annie?" Mr. Lombardi's voice brings me back to the classroom. I look around and realize that my entire class is lined up to go outside. Except for me. "You planning to join us for kickball?"

I drop my pencil and scramble into line. Scratch the rainbow. At this exact moment, my Feelings Folder would definitely be a Mortified Pink. Like the color of my face right now.

We get out to the kickball field, and Mr. Lombardi calls Savannah and Jake to be team captains.

When I hear Savannah's name, I get excited. The only time I get picked first for kickball is when Savannah is captain. You wouldn't know Savannah is good at kickball just from looking at her. She's wearing sparkly purple leggings and tall boots with her white ruffled top. The shirt still has the ketchup stain on it, but it has gotten lighter as the day has gone on, so now you can barely see it. She's always adding unusual accessories to her outfits, and today it's an emerald bandana knotted around her neck like a bow tie. Sometimes the things she chooses even catch on and other kids copy her style. One time she made a bracelet out of dental floss, which I thought was pretty gross, because who wants to wear a tooth gunk cleaner on their arm? But Savannah was somehow able to pull it off. The next day, four other girls were proudly wearing bacteria bracelets.

Before Savannah even opens her mouth, I start to walk over and stand next to her. I'm thinking about how good it will feel to be on the winning team on the last day of school, so I don't even hear Savannah say, "I'll take Phoebe." But what I do hear is Phoebe Rogers gasp and start fanning herself like her name has been called for Miss America, and I freeze. It would be fine if I wasn't standing alone in the awkward, empty space in between the captains and the rest of the class. And if everyone wasn't looking at me. But everyone *is* looking at me, and I can feel the pink making its way back up my cheeks, so I bend down and pluck a dandelion, as if to say, "Yes, yes, simply wandered over to pick this dandelion here. . . . What's that you say? My *best friend* chose someone else first? I didn't even notice!" Then I stand tall, walk back to my place in line, and blow those fluffy wisps off with one smooth puff. I tilt my chin up to the sky, wishing a little that I could float off into the breeze with them. When I finally get myself together, I look Savannah right in the eye. She shrugs and says, "Phoebe kicks it super far!"

I'm trying to decide what color total and complete irritation would be on a Feelings Folder when Jake picks me for his team. "I'll take Marathon Girl," he calls out.

I may not be the fastest, but I can run for a long time. I ran the most laps in the school jog-a-thon this year. Most kids took breaks here and there, but I didn't stop for one second. That was when Jake started calling me "Marathon Girl." Even though I'm proud of the number of laps I ran, I'm not a fan of him calling me that. It's almost as embarrassing as my dad calling me "honeykin" in front of the entire school.

I used to think that being friends with a boy wasn't a big deal, but at some point in fifth grade, things changed. It was like suddenly everyone in my class had "girl" and "boy" tattooed to their forehead, and you were only allowed to talk to people with a matching tattoo. If you dared break that rule, there was always someone watching—someone ready to make obnoxious kissing noises behind your back, or "ship" you. "Shipping" is when someone combines your names to make a single annoying name, like you're in a relation*ship*. The first time Jake called me "Marathon Girl," Phoebe started chanting, "Jannie, Jannie, Jannie!" Jake just laughed it off, but I did *not* think it was funny. Phoebe actually likes the idea of having a boyfriend, and always has a boy that she is "going out" with. I don't know why she calls it that, since the only time they're even seen together is in the moment they decide to "go out." After that, they don't seem to speak to each other at all, and they certainly don't "go out" anywhere.

Today, when Jake says, "I'll take Marathon Girl," he smiles big at me, and as I walk over to his team, I try really hard to hold my face perfectly still. No reaction. It's hard, especially when what I really want to do is scrunch up my nose like my dad's cooking broccoli for dinner again. It's not like smiling is a crime or anything, but Jake's is the kind of smile that is just asking for another round of "Jannie," and if I smile back, I'm toast. I look over at Phoebe and see that she's too busy whispering with Savannah to notice Jake's megawatt grin. For a second I'm relieved, because that means I can stop bracing myself for the teasing that I thought was on its way. But my stomach clenches up again as I begin to wonder if what they're whispering about is me. I throw my shoulders back and take a deep breath. Fine. Savannah will be sorry she didn't pick me when I lead my team to victory with a game-winning home run. Let's play ball.

My team is up first, so we head to the dugout, while Savannah's team spreads out across the field. When it's my turn to kick, I line up behind home plate and try to focus. My team is cheering for me, but the loudest voice I hear is Savannah's. "Let's go, Annie!" She's smiling and giving me a big thumbs-up from the infield. The ball comes bouncy rolling toward me, and I kick it as hard as I can. It's a good, hard kick, and it feels great. The ball flies through the air and I take off toward first base. I'm already picturing the way my team will rush home plate after I round the bases. Maybe they'll even put me up on their shoulders. But as I'm approaching first, I see a streak of pink racing toward the high-flying ball. The cheers of my team shift from excited shouts to a giant disappointed "Oooohhhh" as Phoebe throws herself underneath it.

"You're out! You're out!" Phoebe is yelling and jumping up and down, and her team is running over to her, all high fives and backslaps.

I try to skid to a stop, halfway between first and second base, but I slip and end up down on one knee. Yet again in the awkward empty space. Because of Phoebe. I can feel my eyes start to get warm with tears, and I look down at my knee. It's scraped up, with little specks of blood poking through the skin. It doesn't hurt at all. In fact, I can't even feel it. But the tears are already there, waiting to come out, and it is pretty easy to pretend that it's because of my knee.

Savannah rushes over and helps me up.

"Savannah, why don't you walk Annie to the office to get her knee checked out?" Mr. Lombardi says, handing her a nurse's slip.

"Awww man, not Savannah!" someone from her team yells. "Send somebody else!"

I look at Savannah and see the slightest flicker of hesitation in her eyes. But then she shakes her head, kind of like she's shaking something off. She links her arm in mine and we leave the field together, but I can't help wondering what she was trying to shake.

"You okay?" Savannah asks.

"Sure, yeah. Fine," I say.

"I was saving this for an after-last-day-of-school celebration," Savannah says as she hands me a piece of cinnamon taffy. "But you look like you could use it now."

Cinnamon taffy is my favorite. On my sixth birthday, I had a Princess Puppy Power piñata that was filled with nothing but cinnamon taffy. Dad called that piñata "the piñata of steel," because no matter how hard we whacked it, it wouldn't break. We were swinging away at it in the front yard when Savannah and her mom started moving in next door. Savannah's mom went tripping past us with a giant dollhouse in her arms. It was so tall that she couldn't see over it and almost launched it onto the porch. Dad ran over to help her get it through the front door, and returned with Savannah by his side. "Let's give this little peanut a turn," he suggested. Sure enough, Savannah gave that bat one major league swing and Princess Pomeranian was blasted to smithereens. And then we became best friends. When you're six, I guess all it takes is one person who's willing to give up all her cinnamon taffy, just because she can tell it's your favorite.

We go through the door to the nurse's office and he tells us to sit on the bench and wait while he finishes taking someone's temperature. Savannah clears her throat a few times, and I'm about to ask her if she needs a drink of water when she says, "Would you be okay with me heading back to the kickball game? Since you're actually okay and everything? I want to see if I can get back before it's my turn to kick. Unless you need help with, like, a Band-Aid or something?"

I open my mouth to speak but nothing wants to come out. So instead I shake my head, kind of like now I'm trying to shake something off. I finally push the words out. "No, I don't need any help," I say, "with a Band-Aid." I say "Band-Aid" in an overly dramatic way, and Savannah tilts her head and studies me for a minute, like she does when she's trying to figure out a tough word problem.

"Okay!" She says it extra loud, in her peppy, Savannah way. "See you in a few minutes, then?" I nod and she turns away from me. My nod turns back into a headshake as she goes out the door, and I know exactly what I'm trying to shake off. It's this weird feeling that Savannah is leaving me, and maybe not only for the kickball game. I used to think the best-friends-forever thing was possible, but in moments like these, I start to wonder. Maybe not even the amazing Savannah Summerlyn can be a forever-and-always best friend. She's more like an almost-always best friend. Mom sometimes says, "No one is perfect. That's what makes the world so interesting!" I'm not so sure I'd call it "interesting" when your best friend ditches you, but most of the time, Savannah and I get along like macaroni and cheese, so I guess calling us almost-always best friends works okay. *Best-friends-forever-except-when-playing-kickball* just doesn't have the same ring to it.

When we were six and swinging away at a superhero puppy, it didn't matter who was faster or who kicked the ball harder. Best friends always picked best friends first. Period. There was no almost-always about it. We're clearly not six any-more. And now, on the last day of fifth grade, the day that is supposed to be the best day, we're not even on the same team.

CHAPTER 3

want an accessory
that is both functional
and fashionable?

INTRODUCING

DENTAL DECOR

the jewelry that polishes an outfit and
your pearly whites!

Ewwww. The name change helps, but not enough. I'm sitting alone in Savannah's room, killing time by writing commercials while she finishes her chores. Her mom is a stickler for a clean house, and Savannah gets in trouble if she doesn't get her part done right when she gets home. Almost every day after school, I drop my backpack off at home and then come next door to Savannah's. Since today was the last day of school, it felt like the right thing to do, even though things with us are a little weird. I'm hoping to maybe talk to her about it, but I have to wait until she's done sweeping the kitchen floor. Until then, I'm eating our favorite snack—graham crackers with peanut butter—and wrinventing.

I crumple up the bacteria bracelet idea and turn to a fresh page. I'm looking around the room for inspiration when I see the Heart of a Quail Award on the top shelf of Savannah's bookcase. She must have put it up there while I took my backpack home.

The sun is reflecting off of the glass, which makes it look beautiful, but it gives me a bad feeling in my stomach. I shouldn't have been surprised when Savannah's name was called. And I know I should have felt proud and just plain happy that she won. But instead I felt a kind of barfy-disappointed happy, which is not a good feeling to have. And now that feeling is back.

I stand on my tiptoes and stretch my arm way up to see if I can reach the glass quail. Too high. How did she get it up there? Right next to the book-case is Savannah's dollhouse, and I'm thinking it would make a great stepstool. She's always going on about how it was made in one of those fancy custom dollhouse shops and "crafted with the finest oak," so I'm sure it can support me. I only want to hold the award for a minute, and I can put it back before Savannah finishes her chores. I throw my leg up and rest my foot on the dollhouse's tiny wooden shingles. It's the perfect height. I'll just balance on it long enough to grab the quail and then hop right back down. In the split second before I pull my body up, I start to wonder if maybe this is not such a good idea. But it's too late. As my full weight comes down on the top of the dollhouse, there's a sharp cracking noise. I throw my arm up and grab the trophy just before my foot breaks through the roof. The glass is cool in my hand—the complete opposite of my ankle, which feels like it's on fire.

I roll my ankle around inside the dollhouse and my foot knocks something over. Oops. I hope it wasn't the antique armoire; Savannah will *die* if it's the armoire. She loves to draw out the word—*arrrrrm-wahhhh*—and say it's "vintage." If you ask me, "vintage" is a phony way of saying "old."

I wonder what kind of face Savannah would make if I told her that. Mom says that maybe I wonder too much. Except she calls it "wandering." Like last night when I was supposed to be washing my hair but I accidentally used toothpaste instead of shampoo. She laughed and helped me scrub it out. "Wandering again, Annie?"

But wondering if you've just done the most horrible thing in the history of your friendship is not the good kind of wondering. And wondering how long it will be until that friend finds you in the middle of a sticky situation like this might just be the worst kind of wondering. You sort of do want her to find you, to help you out of it. But you sort of don't, since then you'll have to explain to her how you got stuck in the first place.

CHAPTER 4

If you've never accidentally stepped through the roof of your best friend's dollhouse, you might not know that the moment you crash through it is *not* the worst part. The worst part is when your foot falls asleep because you can't get it back out. Like walking on a porcupine in quicksand. Which I do know, because here I am, foot stuck in a dollhouse, wondering which thing is the most broken—my ankle, the dollhouse, or our friendship. What if Savannah walks in and is so mad that she leaves me stuck? Then I might have to sleep here.

Sleeping in a dollhouse would be kind of exciting if it was a super-big, kid-sized dollhouse. And if I could actually lie down in the canopy bed. Then I guess it would be called a "kidhouse." WAIT. That's a really good idea.

Kids! Are you tired of playing with those old-fashioned dollhouses of Grandma's youth? Parents! Looking for something fresh and exciting to get your kids away from the TV? Well, the search is over, because we've got the solution for you.

Even when I'm in trouble, I can't stop wrinventing. Mr. Lombardi was a great fifth-grade teacher, but he was always telling us that watching TV would rot our brains. What he doesn't get is that I'm not even paying attention to the actual shows. I turn up the volume on the made-for-TV commercials so I can practice my craft. I'm training for my future! So it's kinda like college, and I'm getting good. How else would I know that putting a z on the end of *Kidz* and *Houz* would make it a best seller?

Right when I've decided the only way to get my foot out is to make an even bigger hole in the roof of the dollhouse, I hear Savannah in the hallway. Even if I wasn't in her house, I would know it's her because of the singing. She says her passions are singing, dancing, and eating. She does have a voice that never seems to go off-key, but Mom says eleven years old is awfully young to know what you're passionate about in life. I don't totally agree since I am already practically an expert in my chosen field, but I'm not sure eating can be a life passion, since everybody eats. I dared Savannah once to do all three of her "passions" at the same time, and it did not end well. Let's just say that twirling and chili do not go together.

Or do they . . . WAIT. . . .

Kids, want to eat but can't get that pesky chili to stay in the dish while you boogie down? Parents, are your hungry ballerinas making a mess on your kitchen floor? Stop! There's a better way!

It's the BOWL BUDDY! With one simple snap, you can say good-bye to the sloppy samba and hello to the tidy tango.

I am imagining myself in a headdress of mango and pineapple when the door swings open. "Annie?"

"Over here," I say. It comes out in a sort of squeak, like the kind of sound my little brother's pet mouse, Preston, would make. I get a fuzzy feeling as I think about Evan and wish that I was home with him instead of at Savannah's. Even a little brother who is obsessed with *Alien Hunters* and has a rodent for a best friend sounds better than facing her right now.

Savannah's clearly excited about something, because the words are flying out of her mouth like the house is on fire. ". . . anditwillallbeonlineandtheauditionsareFridayand . . ." At first, she doesn't even seem to notice my completely bizarre and pretzel-like pose in the corner of her room. And then she does. Her eyes get wide. "WHAT DID YOU DO TO MY DOLLHOUSE?"

I'm not sure what to say. I wish I could tell her the truth. That I wanted to hold the Heart of a

Quail Award and pretend to be her. The Amazing Savannah Summerlyn. That I wanted to be the one who was called up to the stage. The one who curtsied as she received it, in a way that wasn't babyish but somehow made everyone laugh and feel good. That I wanted to feel for a moment that people could see me. That I wanted to be the opposite of Invisible Annie.

But I can't. So before I think about what I'm saying, I blurt out, "I saw the most gigantic spider on your wall! I put my foot on the top of the doll-house so I could reach it and then this happened."

Savannah does what she always does when she's frustrated with me. She says my name in a *Really, Annie?* sort of way, like Mom does when I forget to put my clothes in the laundry basket. "Annnnnnieeeee." Then she leans down, mushes her head up against the miniature fireplace, and takes my shoe off so I can lift my leg back through the hole. I'm relieved that Savannah isn't more upset with me. She seems kind of distracted, and whatever it is that's distracting her, I'm grateful for it.

"Lynda will not be pleased," Savannah says, and I am reminded again why she is my almost-always best friend. Lynda is her mom, and Savannah knows it makes me laugh when she calls her mom by her first name. Somehow, even when I'm the one who messed up, and Savannah has every right to be mad at me, *she's* the one making *me* feel better.

"Why do you have the quail?" Savannah asks. Oops. Almost forgot I was holding it. I'm trying to think of a way to respond without telling another lie. It may be because my lie involved an imaginary spider, but all I can think about now is how Dad always goes on about weaving tangled webs when it comes to lying. It started one time after I told him a whopper about why Evan's hair was suddenly and mysteriously shorter on one side. *No! I didn't cut Evan's hair with those scissors on the table that have hair the exact color of Evan's stuck in them! I would never!* (I did.) My punishment was to sit and listen to him read a forever-long poem by a guy named Sir Walter Scott. At first I thought the writer's name was actually "Sir," but Dad explained that it was a British thing and giving someone the title "Sir" meant that some bigwig in Britain thought Walter Scott was an amazing poet. So in Britain he's called Sir Walter Scott, but around our house, Dad just calls him "Uncle Walt." Like, when he suspects one of us isn't telling the whole truth he raises an eyebrow and asks, "What would Uncle Walt say?" Uncle Walt's poem is full of old-timey words like *'twas* and *quell,* so it is pretty hard to understand. But I do remember the part about the lies. "Oh what a tangled web we weave, / When first we practice to deceive!" That means that once you tell one lie, you end up having to tell more lies so you don't get caught in the first one. And it ends up being a giant confusing web. I'm envisioning myself getting slowly wrapped up in the thin sticky strings when Savannah saves me.

"If you had tried to smash a spider with that, there would have been a hole in my wall, too!"

"Totally," I say, relieved. "That would have been stupid." Not a lie, but I suspect Uncle Walt would still not approve.

"Annie!" Savannah says. "You almost made me forget the thing I ran in to tell you! I have the most exciting news *ever*."

"Well, tell me, then!" I say, shaking out my sleepy leg.

If I had known what was coming, that behind her excitement there would be something that would change our friendship forever, I might have worked harder to let her forget.

CHAPTER 5

Savannah waves a flier in my face. "Look what
came in the mail today!"

ATTENTION, LOCAL KIDS WITH TALENT!
Come audition this Friday for:
THE CAT'S MEOW
A web show starring YOU!
For kids and by kids, THE CAT'S MEOW will feature
News
Events
Products
ALL JUST FOR KIDS

"*The Cat's Meow*?" I ask. "Does that mean it's
an animal show?" I'm imagining myself under the

big top, taming wild beasts in the center ring. That could be fun, and I definitely think I could pull off the outfit—a top hat and a coat with tails. I hop onto her bed and stand up. "What do you think of this?" I put on my best TV commercial voice for Savannah and begin, "*Come one, come all! Come see Annie Brown, Animal Ace, as she trains the most frightening felines in the forest!*"

"Annie!" Savannah, who is used to me breaking out into my latest wrinvention, tries to get me to stop, but I'm on a roll.

"*Come watch the wildlife whiz perform feats that will astonish and amaze you! She'll conquer the colossal cougar and tame the terrifying tiger with bravery beyond compare!*"

"Annie Brown! Focus!" Savannah puts on her serious voice so I give in, even though I was just getting started. "It's not an animal show," she continues. "'The cat's meow' is a saying from back when all the movies were black and white, which I only know because of all the completely ancient movies my mom makes me watch with her. They would say something was 'the cat's meow' when it was really awesome. Like if you heard a song you loved, you would say, 'That song is the cat's meow.'"

"Seriously?" I ask, giggling a little. "What about other animals? Would they say 'it's the dog's bark'? Or 'the horse's neigh'? Or 'the rooster's cock-a-doodle-doo'?"

Savannah giggles, too. "No," she says, "but they did say, 'That's the bee's knees!'"

"No they didn't!" I'm holding my side now; I'm laughing so hard. "Do bees even have knees?" Savannah's laughing uncontrollably now, too, and throws herself down on her bed. Somehow, even after the drama of the dollhouse, we are still able to go right back to our friendship happy place, making each other laugh in Savannah's room.

Once we've calmed down, Savannah says, "Isn't it exciting, Annie? With your made-for-TV commercial voice you'll be the perfect host, and I can be a featured performer. I'm already working on my routine. Watch!" She bops side to side, and her blond curls bounce in time. She has annoyingly perfect hair. It's a little bit like Rapunzel's, except not quite so long. She can toss it from shoulder to shoulder and she has these wispy tendrils that she twists around her finger when she gets bored. My hair, on the other hand, is annoyingly annoying. Brown. Straight. Short.

I once tried to convince Mom to order me some Lovely Locks.

Tired of hair that won't grow beyond your shoulders? Wishing you had supermodel gorgeous tresses? Never fear, Lovely Locks are here! Clip them on and you'll have people admiring your long, luxurious hair in no time!

But even though we could have had them in three easy payments of only $9.95, Mom said no.

I reach up and touch my hair. Still flat as a pancake. Savannah must know I'm thinking about my hair because she almost shouts, "Oh, Annie! You have to let me do your hair for the audition. I watched the best video online about how to do an upside-down french braid, and I know it would be perfect. Let's practice now!"

Savannah has me lie down on her bed and hang my head over the side so that she can start the braid at the nape of my neck. She's lucky I don't have a sensitive head, because she's pulling it so tight I'm pretty sure a giant chunk of hair is going to come off in her hand. I kinda want to tell her to forget it, but she's halfway through at this point, so I bite my lip a little and stick it out.

"There, it's perfect!" She stands me in front of the mirror but keeps her hand over my eyes. "Introducing the new host of *The Cat's Meow* . . . Annie Brown!" She drops her hand from my face and I stare into the mirror. I can't see the braid at all, since it's at the back of my head, but what I do see is that when she finished the braid, she put the leftover hair in a ponytail on top of my head. Like, directly on top of my head. Like, is that a chocolate fountain or a fifth grader? And then she topped it off with an enormous hot pink bow. I look like a giant Valentine's Day present.

"Ummmm . . ."

"It's the pink, isn't it?" Savannah says. "I know it's not your favorite, but I wanted something that would really make an impact, you know? Something that will make you stand out from the crowd!"

I have never liked pink. Not hot pink, light pink, or any pink in between. In first grade, we did one of those get-to-know-you activities where you go around and everyone says their favorite color. I was so excited to share mine, because my grammy has a bright orange room in her basement and I love it there. It always feels so welcoming, like it's waiting for kids to come in and be happy in it. So when it was my turn, I said, "Orange!"

Big mistake. Phoebe made a frowny face and said, "Ewwww!" and suddenly I felt like I had said something very wrong. It was no surprise when Phoebe announced that her favorite color was pink—she was wearing an outfit so pink and froofy it looked like cotton candy threw up all over her. Most of the girls in our class said pink. At least Savannah had the creativity to say her favorite color was "blush." Savannah was helping her mom pick paint colors for their house at the time, and all the paint colors had funky names like Cerulean Sky and Marigold Butter. I've always thought that it would be an amazing job to be a paint namer. I'm not even sure that's a real job, but it should be. I even wrinvented an official job title for myself: Annie Brown, Hue Guru. I had to use a thesaurus to come up with something more exciting than "Color Expert." And Hue Guru is super fun to say.

Want to spruce up your house with a fresh coat of paint? Are you tired of choosing from plain, boring colors? Well, look no further, the HUE GURU is here to help!

The HUE GURU

knows that red, orange, yellow, blue, and green are not all the colors of the rainbow! Freshen up your living room with her signature dark maroon, the ferocious Lion's Blood! Breathe new life into that stinky bathroom with her pale sea-foam Lime Dream Supreme! Create a whole new look for your bedroom with a lovely lavender, the HUE GURU's favorite, Luscious Lilac Garden.

If I had a pink paint color, I might name it "Cotton Candy Barf." I'm pretty sure it would not be a best seller.

I don't do pink and I usually don't do bows, so let's just say that wearing a giant hot pink bow on top of my head like I'm trying to flag down a passing airplane is not my idea of a good time.

"Let me think about it," I finally say. I want my audition to be memorable, but I'm not sure this noggin sprout is what I want to be remembered for. Maybe I can talk to Mom again about the Lovely Locks. I could explain to her that I need to look professional, and everyone knows that on-air personalities have to have great hair.

"*The Cat's Meow* is what you've been practicing for your whole life," Savannah says. "It couldn't be more perfect for you." She gets into her cheerleading ready position, with her neck tall and her hands folded neatly behind her back. Her arms swing to her sides and she calls out, "Ready, OKAY! Give me an *A*! Give me an *N*! Give me an *N-I-E*! What's that spell? *ANNIE!* Who's gonna win? *ANNIE!*"

I smile and join in, stepping side to side. My rhythm is off, and I keep stepping the wrong direction at the wrong time and calling out the wrong letters. But Savannah doesn't care that I'm out of step, or awkward, or that I can't even spell my own name. We just laugh. Together. I guess the last day of school wasn't so bad after all.

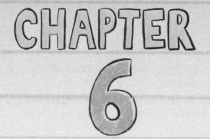

CHAPTER 6

"Friday, huh?" Dad says.

"Friday . . . hmm . . . let me think . . . Friday . . . ," Mom says.

"Zakow!" Evan is zapping flying aliens that are circling my chair. I am trying to sit still and not whap him on the head, because I really, really want my parents to say yes. Sometimes I wish I had a sister instead. If I had a sister, she would be helping me convince them right now. We'd be partners in crime. And I would tell her all about *The Cat's Meow*, and she would pinkie promise with a kiss not to tell my secrets. Instead, I've got the Martian Muncher.

Mom and Dad go on for a while about all the things they need to do Friday, which I don't get because they both work on fold-up tables in the extra room, so it's not like they need to be somewhere.

Dad writes lots of stories that not many people read. Usually his stories involve elves and trolls and magical creatures whose names I can't pronounce. But sometimes he writes funny stories. Those are my favorite. Last week he read us a story about a chipmunk who wished she was a poodle. After he reads a story to us, he asks us if it's a "keeper" or a "stinker." That chipmunk was a keeper.

While it's fun to hear his stories, sometimes I wish he had a normal job like my other friends' parents. If Dad worked in an office on the top floor of a giant skyscraper, then he could wear a dapper suit with a shimmery tie. Yes, a teal shimmery tie would be perfect. And a briefcase that he needs a secret password to unlock.

Mom needs all kinds of passwords for her job. Taking care of other people's money means a ton of scrunched eyebrows and zillions of numbers scrawled on scratch paper. She's a real whiz at math. Sometimes, when she's not home, I have to ask Dad for help with my math homework. Usually he just stares at the page, clears his throat, and says something like, "Let's see here, looks like your teacher has assigned confusometrics again!" According to him, my teacher assigns confusometrics and perplexometry on a regular basis. Then, he waves his arms around in the air like he's doing some sort of crazy dance move and says, "Time to summon the math genie!" What this actually means is that he's going to search the Internet for the math problem I'm working on. I guess I could go straight to the laptop myself, but that wouldn't be as much fun.

Mom is super smart when it comes to numbers. But her job involves *lots* of sighing. I have told her that instead of crunching numbers, she should be making fancy cupcakes in a cozy shop called Bella's Bakery. She loves baking because, as she puts it, baking is really just math. She gets so excited when she talks about it. "Making cupcakes is a formula! Stick to the formula, and you can make any kind of cupcake in the universe!" I don't think she understands that kids don't want cupcakes to be about math. We want them to be about cake. And frosting. Lots of frosting. Her cupcakes are the best, though. She likes to experiment with unusual flavors. Lemon Ginger was a keeper. Peppered Maple was a stinker. If she owned a bakery, then she could wear a frilly apron and chef's hat to work instead of her blue fuzzy pants and slipper socks. I even wrote the perfect commercial for her.

Sick of those powdery cake box flavors? Vanilla and chocolate? Boor-ing! And what kind of flavor is Yellow Cake, anyway? Come and meet Bella, the Queen of Baking!

Surprise your senses with our Salted Caramel Supreme! Tickle your tongue with our Triple Truffle Treat! Cheer up your chums with our Cherry Cheesecake Chunk!

Get the royal treatment at

Bella's Bakery,

where our amazing tastes match your amazing taste buds!

But there are no chef's hats or shimmery ties going on in this house right now, just a never-ending discussion about Friday.

"Friday, huh?" Dad says again.

"Yeppers," I say, trying to charm him with one of his own silly made-up words.

"I think we could make Friday work," Mom says.

I'm in such a good mood that I don't fuss at all when Evan begs me to play Galaxy Guys. I stomp down the hall like a zombie while he chases me. I even let him capture me, and act out a long, drawn-out death scene. It's kind of fun, and besides, I figure it's good practice for Friday. My favorite commercials on TV are the ones that have the most over-the-top actors in them—people that seem so crazy passionate about their product you can't help but want to buy it. So I have to bring my most enthusiastic and dramatic self to that audition, because this is the opportunity I've been waiting for. I can't blow it. Savannah was right, *The Cat's Meow* is perfect for me, which means that Friday is a super important day. Maybe the most important day of my life. My future begins on Friday!

Friday, huh?

Yeppers.

CHAPTER 7

The day after the last day of school is also pretty great. You might think it would feel like a regular Saturday, but it doesn't, because it's a Saturday that leads into a giant stretch of days that feel like more wonderful Saturdays. Today is the last game of my spring soccer league, so I don't get to sleep in, but I don't even mind. Dad pokes his head into our bedroom super early and wakes Evan and me up by singing some song about school being out for summer. He's using his phone as a pretend microphone and whipping his head around like he has long rocker hair.

My good mood from last night has carried over to this morning, so I play along, pretending to be the drummer in his rock band. Evan hops out of bed and joins in by strumming his air guitar. As the song ends, I fling my comforter off and throw up jazz hands for a little finale flair. Dad protests, "Rockers don't do jazz hands!" But he and Evan join in anyway, just as Mom comes into the room. She grins at the three of us waving our arms around.

"Sorry to interrupt your musical production, but it's time to get ready for soccer." She tosses my uniform to me, and I jump out of bed to get ready.

We're supposed to get to the field thirty minutes before the game to warm up, but Mom absolutely hates to be late, so we are always there way early. We walk over to our field and I see that Jake Ramirez's team is playing the game before ours. Evan heads over to the playground with Dad while Mom and I find a small patch of open grass and kick around the soccer ball we brought from home. I pay real close attention to which part of my foot hits the ball when I pass it. Mom's a perfectionist when it comes to soccer technique, since she played in college. Inside of the foot for short, controlled passes. Contact at the laces for shots on goal. Knee over the ball. Toe down. It's a lot to keep track of! But Mom's a real pro, so I do try to follow her advice. Well, most of the time, anyway.

I've always thought that she should make one of those instructional videos, teaching kids how to play soccer.

Want to be an Olympic soccer player? Trying your best, but feeling like a real klutz on the soccer field? Never fear, THE KICK CHICK is here! In her series of three instructional videos, she'll teach you the skills you need to become the best!

Pass like a pro. Shoot like a star! Dribble like a doofus no more. THE KICK CHICK will take your soccer game from goofy to groovy in no time at all.

When I first started playing soccer, Jake and I were on the same team, and Mom was our coach. But that was way back in the days when boys and girls played together and everyone ran wild around the field, bounding after the ball like dogs playing fetch. I loved that kind of soccer. Running free and not worrying about the rules. Every once in a while, a kid would catch the ball with their hands and run around the field with it, and everyone would laugh. Now, parents and coaches are way more intense. They want us to learn technique, to play positions, and—most importantly—to win. When we were little, they didn't even keep score! But I guess that's the thing about getting older. It seems like there's always a right and a wrong way to do things, and everyone keeps score.

I use my left foot and one-touch pass the ball back to Mom. I'm working on my left foot, but right now it's kinda terrible, and the ball veers way off to the side of her. I'm about to chase after it when I see Jake intercept it and start dribbling back over to us. His game must have ended. "Nice left, Marathon Girl," he says. As usual, he's smiling. Sometimes his smile confuses me, because I can't tell if he's being serious or messing with me, but this time I know he's being sarcastic since it was not a nice pass at all. I roll my eyes.

"Jake! I'm so glad you're here!" Mom says. "Take my place, will ya? This old lady needs a break."

I'm about to object, since I'm not sure I want to be left alone with Jake. But then I think about how my mom actually is sorta old and might really need a break. After all, she did just turn thirty-nine. Next year, she'll be forty, and then I'll really have to be careful.

Jake agrees and takes Mom's spot across the grass from me. I'm thinking this might not be so bad. Jake is a pretty good soccer player, and we can have a perfectly good time kicking the ball around without even talking. Our moms have been friends since we were born, so we used to play together a lot. I have memories of eating vanilla wafers on my checkerboard carpet while our parents drank coffee and chatted about preschool. Sometimes we would play one-on-one soccer in the backyard, and whoever lost had to spin around twenty times and then try to walk in a straight line to the garage. Jake used to get so dizzy he could hardly take a single step before falling down. I would crack up and Jake would clutch his stomach, threatening to puke all over the place. But as we've gotten older, our moms have started making lunch dates while we're at school, so we don't hang out as much.

Sometimes I wish we could go back to those cookie-eating days—the days when I didn't have to worry about getting teased for our friendship. Even our parents tease us now, which is terrible because aren't they supposed to be setting a good example? But I've heard my mom and Mrs. Ramirez laughing about how Jake and I got "married" once at recess in preschool, and Mrs. Ramirez said she kept a note

I wrote Jake that same year, "just in case." I have no idea what the note says, but it makes me super nervous because back in preschool I told everyone I loved them, including my stuffed bunny, and my teacher, Mrs. Cleary. I even used to tell the ants that lived near the garbage cans in our backyard that I loved them before I had to go inside for the night. So I'm sure the note says something completely mortifying. And I don't know why she still has it. "Just in case"? Just in case of what? Just in case she needs to send an innocent eleven-year-old girl into hiding for the rest of her life?

More of my teammates are arriving, and my coach calls us over. Jake puts his hand out as I run past, and I high-five him. "Go get 'em, MG," he says. I don't say anything back, and am surprised to see Jake and his mom still standing on the sideline as the whistle blows for the start of the game.

It's our last game, and it's a great one. We win 1–0, and I had the assist. I lead our team in assists, but that just means I passed the ball to the person who scored the goal. And obviously it's an important part of the game, but it's not the part that people talk about. They talk about who scored the goal. And everyone cheers when it happens, but it's usually for the person who kicked the ball in. Today, after our team scores, I hear Jake's voice. "Great pass, Marathon Girl!" And even though I always try so hard not to react when he calls me that, I can't help grinning at him, because I can't believe that someone actually noticed the assist. So I grin like crazy, and don't even care that it's at Jake, because it feels amazing to be seen. And I start thinking that maybe the person who chose a troubadour as a mascot knew what they were doing. Because right now, I'm the warrior and Jake is my troubadour, and it feels great. All he's missing is the tights.

CHAPTER 8

"Signing off, this is Annie Brown for *The Cat's Meow*."

It's Thursday, and Savannah and I have been practicing all week. Right now, I'm wondering what my parents were thinking when they named me. They must have been feeling extremely uncreative on the day I was born. My actual name is Ann. It's only three letters long, and two of them are the same! Is that the best they could do? Dad always says we are "spicing it up" by calling me *Annie*. But putting an *eee* sound on the end of a name doesn't make it more interesting. I wish I had an elegant name, like Evianna Izabella. Or at least Alexandra. And maybe the first name wouldn't be so bad if my last name wasn't equally boring. Brown. Ann Brown. Two measly syllables. So forgettable.

Savannah has the perfect name. Her mom sure knew what she was doing when she picked it. If Savannah feels like being elegant, she is Savannah Summerlyn. If she doesn't, she's S-squared. That's what I call a great nickname.

"Maybe I should come up with a stage name," I say to Savannah.

"Annie! Focus! We have exactly one day to get you ready for the spotlight. Stop worrying about your name!"

Savannah wants me to audition with a scene from her favorite TV show, *Tabitha with a Twist*. It's a show about Tabitha, who on the outside looks like an ordinary girl, but is secretly a magic fairy who can grant wishes. "It's perfect!" she tells me. "Everyone loves Tabitha, and she's super spunky, just like you!"

But I have other ideas. "I wrote a commercial for the audition," I say. "Listen."

"Are you a sea-life lover, tired of dealing with stinky fish food and murky water? want an aquarium, but don't want the extra work and expense involved in taking care of it? we've got the product for you!

Introducing

the tankless, waterless aquarium you hang on your wall. You can try FISHLIGHT today for only $19.95!"

I got the idea for Fishlight after Evan's fish, Squishy, died. The big problem was that Evan wanted to teach Squishy tricks, but the only thing that goldfish did was swim around in circles all day long. Evan finally got tired of it and took the little guy out of the water to see if he was as squishy as he looked. That was an even bigger problem. I figure a Fishlight is a great idea not only because fake light-up fish would look amazing hanging on the wall, but because it would be saving the lives of real fish all over the world.

I wonder how a Fishlight would look on the wall of my bedroom. I wish I had my own room, but I don't. I have to share it with the Alien Zapper. Evan's actually not too bad, especially because he is a little bit of a neat freak and will even clean up my side of the room just because it makes him feel better. And I would never tell him this, but last month when he spent the night at his friend Charlie's house, it was so quiet in our room that I had trouble falling asleep. I can't believe it but I think I missed the little snore-sigh sound he makes when he first falls asleep. So I guess the only reason I want my own room is because I can't decorate this one the way I want. Mom and Dad say we have to keep it "neutral," which, if you ask me, is just another way of saying "boring." Right now our room has yellow walls with checked curtains and twin beds with matching yellow quilts. What I really want is an undersea animal theme, but with only beautiful sea creatures, like dolphins and mermaids. No octopuses allowed. And turquoise walls. Yup, a Fishlight full of miniature dolphins on a turquoise wall would be perfection.

Savannah is still trying to talk me into reciting the script she printed out for me.

She wants me to say, "Swirl, girl, let the magic unfurl!" This is Tabitha's signature line, and I try it but it doesn't feel right. It sort of tumbles out of my mouth in a weird way. Plus, Savannah wants me to sashay around the room while I say it. She demonstrates for me, but the hop-skip-glide requires a level of gracefulness that I clearly don't have.

It's not working. I turn back to my Fishlight script. I take out my orange marker and add to the end:

But wait! There's more! Call now and we'll double the offer. Order FISHLIGHT in the next fifteen minutes and get a second FISHLIGHT for free!

Much better. I put on my best TV announcer voice and practice again.

That night I dream about the audition. In my dream, the people in charge of *The Cat's Meow* stop the auditions after hearing me introduce the Fishlight.

"Send the rest of the kids home!" they say.

"We have found the host of our dreams!" they say.

"Fishlights for everyone!" they say.

And I feel sure that it's a sign. That for once in my life, everything will go the way it is supposed to.

CHAPTER 9

"Ugh, it just feels so . . . scritchy!" *Scritchy* is another one of Dad's wrinvented words, and it's a keeper. A combination of *scratchy* and *itchy*, it perfectly describes how I feel wiggling around in the red ruffled top that Savannah brought over for me to wear to the audition today. She says that red will really "pop" on camera.

But the ruffles are extremely *scritchy*, which means I am clawing at my neck, which means my neck is now blotchy and also red. The sort of red you really *don't* want to pop on camera. I take the top off and reach into my closet for my lucky sweater. It's the color of butter—pale yellow—with a lavender heart on the pocket. The best part about it is the chunky buttons down the front, which are great for fiddling with when I'm nervous about something. Last month I wore it during the school spelling bee and twisted the top button completely off. I had to go without it for two weeks until Mom finally had time to sew the button back on. That was when I had the idea for Sticky Buttons.

Buttons on your favorite shirt fall off constantly? Don't have time to tinker with a needle and thread? Sew no more with STICKY BUTTONS!

STICKY BUTTONS

attach to your most-loved clothes with a super glue-like grip. Keep extras in your pockets or purse. Keep some in your car, just in case!

Don't wait. Call or click now and get STICKY BUTTONS shipped right to your door for our lowest price ever!

I slip the sweater on and tug at the buttons a tiny bit. They're good and tight. Phew.

"This is what I'm wearing," I tell Savannah.

"That old thing again?" she says.

Savannah has this poster on her wall that says, *Good friends are like stars. You can't always see them, but you know they're always there.* I get what it's trying to say, but I've always thought it was kind of creepy sounding. Like they might be hiding in your closet at night, watching you sleep. And when your almost-always best friend lives next door, you already see them *every* day, even on the days when you think it might feel okay to not see them. And then there are days like this one. Days when something big is happening, and you think you want them there with you, because they are like this bright constellation that shines all around you and makes you feel good about the world. But then they say something that bugs you and you think that maybe you'd like them to be a star like the poster says. Something you can't see. At least until they stop calling your favorite sweater "that old thing."

"This old thing is perfection," I say firmly. I don't want her to think she can talk me out of it. She's great at talking me into things that I don't want to do, so I have to bo oonfidcnt. Savannah must get the message, because she drops it.

In the car on our way to the audition, Savannah belts out the *Tabitha* theme song:

"She's a girl with a secret, see if you can keep it, fairy magic's on the list, Ta-bith-aaaaa, with a twist!"

The thought of singing in front of anyone, even my almost-always best friend, scares the rice and beans out of me. But Savannah loves to sing and doesn't care who hears her. I laugh as she dips her shoulders left and right, dancing to the silly *Tabitha* song. As we walk into the studio together, she grabs my hand. She squeezes it, and the nervousness seems to whirl right out of me, like water down the bathtub drain.

My buttons might survive, after all.

CHAPTER 10

The first person I see when we walk into the room is Jake. Lately, it seems like Jake shows up everywhere. We live in the same neighborhood, so I don't mean it in some crazy stalkerish way. And I suppose, since we've known each other forever, that's the way it's always been. I've just never noticed it so much before. Jake's always been there, always smiling at me. I guess there are worse things. He's wearing an old soccer jersey, and it makes me wonder if maybe there's a sports segment of *The Cat's Meow*. Since Mom loves soccer so much, we watch a lot of it on TV. It's the one thing I like almost as much as commercials. I think I would be pretty good at being a sports commentator. The key is that you have to write in funny jokes while also telling people what happened in the most dramatic way possible.

Number 13 clears the ball out of the goal box, saving her team from what appeared to be certain defeat. And this pass has had a ripple effect, like waves that rock the water when your uncle Bernie does a cannonball into Grandma's pool. Ka-blam! One big defensive move, and this team has come alive!

I look over and see Jake's older sister, Riley. So that's why he's here. She's practicing a scene from *Aladdin*. She's the genie, and she's good. Funny. But even funnier is watching her dad. He is sitting across from her, mouthing the words along with her, and stretching his arms out in front of him like he's directing an orchestra. I elbow Savannah and nod over to him. We both giggle.

"Sign in, please." A lady with a layer of hot pink peeking out from underneath her blond hair waves us over. Her name tag says RAINA, written with a little heart over the *i*. The studio is not as fancy as I had imagined it. It reminds me of the waiting room in my dentist's office. There are a couple of lines of chairs, and all but one of them is full. We give Mom the chair and find a spot on the floor.

"*Tabitha* is right here," Savannah says, tapping the folder in her hands, "in case you change your mind."

The truth is that I am getting a little bit tired of Savannah bringing up *Tabitha*. But Mom says that there are moments we have to ask ourselves if telling the exact truth to our friends is the right choice. She said that even Uncle Walt would agree that we don't always have to say *everything* we're thinking. We talked about it after I told one of my soccer teammates she was too slow. "You're supposed to beat the other person to the ball," I told her, and then I suggested she might like swimming better than soccer. I thought I was being helpful, but her parents didn't see it that way.

Since I'm pretty sure this is a moment I should keep the *exact* truth to myself, I smile and say, "I'm good with Fishlight."

"All right, time to get started!" Raina gets everyone's attention. "We've put you in random order, and will be calling you one at a time into that room." She points to the door on the left. "If you've brought a résumé, you can hand it to Mr. Sharp, the director, once you enter."

My eyes widen and I give Mom a panicked look. "Résumé?"

"It's a list of your credentials," she whispers. "Things you've done before that would help you know how to do this job." She shrugs and waves her hand around like she's swatting a bug. She's trying to tell me not to worry about it, but it's not working.

I'm worried.

I start to worry even more when I hear the first name Raina calls. "Phoebe Rogers," she says, and from across the room I see a cloud of pink pop into view.

"Here I am!" Phoebe says eagerly.

This is not a good sign.

"Let's wait over there for Phoebe to come out," Savannah suggests. "Then she can tell us what will happen when we go in!"

While we wait for Phoebe, I practice my Fish-light commercial about twenty-seven more times.

When Phoebe finally comes out, she has a gigantic smile on her face. Savannah runs over and gives her a hug. "How did it go?" she asks.

I'm trying to listen to Phoebe, because I'm sure it's important information.

"The director was very impressed with my résumé," she says.

Information that might help me when it's my turn.

"Because you know I did that car commercial for Burt Baxter Ford a few years ago."

I literally have to freeze my eyeballs in their sockets because what they want to do is roll big-time. I'm not sure it counts as "doing a commercial," when you're a two-year-old that waves from the back of a new car in the last three seconds of an ad for a local car lot. Plus, Burt Baxter is her uncle, so it *really* doesn't count.

But I can't focus very well because I keep thinking about how Savannah gave Phoebe that giant hug when she came out. Like they were friends or something.

". . . and the producers are all so friendly! It was a real breeze," Phoebe says. Her mom starts waving at her from the doorway. "Gotta go," she says, and gives Savannah *another* hug. Then she stops in front of me. "Um, so, good luck, Annie. Break a leg!"

While I know that "break a leg" means good luck in the theater, I can't help but feel that, coming from Phoebe, maybe it doesn't mean good luck at all. And while I'm pretty sure that she would feel bad if I actually broke my leg, something inside me feels like she might be okay with a sprain or a fracture. It's not a good feeling.

I practice some more.

Savannah and I play hangman on the back of the *Tabitha* script.

We pop balloons for points on Mom's iPhone.

Seriously? Am I going to be *last*?

Finally, Raina calls my name. Savannah and I both stand up to go in. "Which one of you is Annie?" Raina asks.

I raise my hand, and Savannah chimes in, "I'm her manager."

"Well." Raina smiles. "We wouldn't want to send Annie in without her manager! Go ahead."

I take a deep breath. Out of the corner of my eye I see Jake giving me a thumbs-up sign. I pretend like I don't see him, because I already feel barfy and

I'm sure if I turn toward him he's going to call me "Marathon Girl," and then I'll feel even barfier. My legs are a little shaky, but I take one step and the rest of my body seems to follow. I try to give Mom a little smile as we walk away, but the corners of my mouth seem to have forgotten how to turn up.

Here we go.

CHAPTER 11

The room is mostly empty, except for a table with two people sitting behind it. The man, who I'm guessing is the director, Mr. Sharp, looks nothing like I imagined him. I thought he would look artistic, and maybe talk with a French accent. And I definitely thought he would be wearing a hat, like maybe one of those mushroom-shaped ones that painters wear, tilted a little to the side. But he is none of those things. He actually looks a little bit like my dad.

The woman with him speaks first. "Hello there," she says, holding out her hand. "My name is Jane

O'Malley, and I'm one of the producers of *The Cat's Meow*. You can call me Jane."

I know I'm supposed to step forward and shake her hand, but I'm frozen in place. My mouth is so dry that I try to swallow but can't. Savannah tries to push me toward them, but I don't budge.

"*Annnnnnieeeee . . .*," Savannah says under her breath. There is a long silence. Too long. Like a-hundred-degrees-outside-so-hot-you-want-to-cry-waiting-for-the-car-AC-to-kick-in kind of loooooong. Finally, Savannah steps forward and shakes Jane's hand.

"Hello, hello!" Savannah says in an overly cheery voice. "Good to meet you! My name is Savannah and I am here with my friend Annie, your next host of *The Cat's Meow*! Annie is gathering her thoughts, and then she will be ready to audition for you— won't you, Annie?" Savannah gives me that *Really, Annie?* look. "You are going to be amazed by her commercial, one she wrote for this very occasion, about a fabulous new product called the Fishlight!"

Fishlight?

Fishlight.

Fishlight!

I imagine a giant glowing aquarium on the wall of a fabulous new turquoise room, and it's like I can breathe again. I look at Savannah. She saved me, big-time.

"Thank you, Savannah!" I say it like a TV anchor who has just wrapped up a conversation with a reporter at the scene. I act natural, like Savannah and I had planned that introduction from the start. I put on my most professional voice and begin. "Are you a sea-life lover, tired of dealing with stinky fish food and murky water?"

I make eye contact with Mr. Sharp and speak slowly, clearly. "Want an aquarium, but don't want the extra work and expense involved in taking care of it?"

I'm hoping to see some flicker of *wow* on his face, but all he does is nod a few times. "Well, I've got the perfect product for you . . . introducing FISHLIGHT, the tankless, waterless aquarium you hang on your wall. You can try FISHLIGHT today for only $19.95!"

Nothing. His lips stay in a perfectly straight line. I feel like I should do something else to get his attention. Now I'm wishing I really was a troubadour, because I think a song and dance might do the trick. Too bad I can't carry a tune. I'm so bad that I once wrote a song about not being able to sing. It was to the tune of "Twinkle, Twinkle, Little Star."

Want to hear a little song?

Trust me, you are very wrong.

Ears will bleed and babies cry

When they hear me wailing by.

Run away, don't take a chance

Or you'll have to watch me dance.

Dad said the song was wonderfully ironic. I didn't know it was a compliment, since when I hear the word *ironic* it makes me think of *bubonic* or *demonic*, neither of which are good things. Dad was surprised that I knew what those other words meant, but somehow didn't know that ironic is when you say something and want it to mean the opposite of what it really means. Like when you name your gigantic dog "Tiny." That's ironic.

I do wonder if being ironic would impress Mr. Sharp. But something tells me this is not the right time for my troubadour debut.

So I do the only thing I can think of at this point, and get louder.

I start the final lines, and now I'm practically shouting. "But wait! There's more! Call now and we'll double the offer. Order FISHLIGHT in the next fifteen minutes and get a second FISHLIGHT for free!"

I was wrong. Mr. Sharp doesn't look like my dad at all. Dad would have smiled, laughed, and even clapped at the end. Mr. Sharp just nods.

When I'm done, Jane says, "Thank you, Annie. We'll be in touch."

Mr. Sharp is silent. Until we turn to leave, and

he says, "Wait a minute, now. I'd like to hear from Savannah."

"Um," Savannah hesitates. "I was planning to come back next month for the featured guest auditions?"

"What's that in your hand?" Mr. Sharp asks.

"Oh, this is a scene from *Tabitha with a Twist*. It's a backup audition," Savannah says, "for Annie."

"Perfect. We'll hear that, then. Please begin."

Savannah looks at me, eyes wide.

I want to scream NOOOOO!

I want to grab the paper out of her hands and tear it into a million tiny pieces.

I want to put another hole in the roof of her precious dollhouse.

But instead, I follow Mr. Sharp's example, and nod. But it's an ironic nod, because it's the exact opposite of what I mean.

Savannah reads from the *Tabitha* script with expression and enthusiasm. She sings, "Swirl, girl, let the magic unfurl!" with perfect pitch. And she sashays gracefully as she sings it.

Mr. Sharp smiles.

Savannah is light-up-his-face wonderful.

Savannah has the voice of an angel.

Savannah is perfect, and once again I stand off to the side as her fans clap for her.

Jane says, "Wow, what a wonderful stage presence you have! Great job, Savannah!" Savannah looks over at me with a hesitant smile, and I somehow manage to echo Jane's words.

"Great job, Savannah!"

Savannah comes over and links her arm in mine. As we walk out of the room together, she whispers to me, "That was okay, right? We're okay?"

I know what I'm supposed to say, so I say it. "Yeah, we're okay."

But it's not true.

I am not okay.

What would Uncle Walt say?

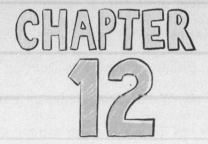

CHAPTER 12

"Wow," Savannah says as we climb into the car with Mom. "That was weird!"

"Mmm-hmm," I say, but inside I'm thinking that it didn't have to be weird. I'm remembering this time my parents took us to the aquarium. Savannah and I wanted to search for mermaids, but instead we found a bunch of unusual sea creatures, and boy, were they weird. The red-lipped batfish, with its bright ruby lipstick was weird. The goblin shark, with its scaly skin and buggy eyes was weird. The blobfish, with its big round nose and sad-looking face was *really* weird. We *ooohed* and *aaahed* over the unavoidable weirdness of these creatures, who were destined to be part of these curious species. But this weirdness with Savannah is not the unavoidable kind. If that audition was weird, it's because she made it that way. Savannah had a choice. She could have walked out of there without auditioning, but she didn't. This is no blobfish.

Savannah is so chatty, I don't even think she notices that I am silent. I'm silent, like Mr. Sharp after my audition, for a long time.

"Oh, Annie, you did such a good job, you knocked their socks off with your commercial! I can't wait to show up tomorrow and see your name on the list. What a great summer this is going to be! I wonder what the different themes of the shows will be? I hope there are some that are about singing and dancing. You and I could work on a routine together, or maybe that could be a segment on the show, where I teach you ballet, or tap! Ooooh, wouldn't that be cool?"

It's quiet for a moment, and I think that maybe if I focus on breathing, we can make it home without any problems. But then Savannah says something that for some reason makes me feel like my insides are going to explode right out of me.

"That was so much fun, don't-cha think, Annie?"

Before I know it, the words are spilling out of me, in a terrible voice that I don't even recognize as my own. "Of course *you* thought that was fun; everything is so easy for you—you don't even have to try and it's super ANNOYING."

"ANNIE!" Mom scolds, but I don't even care. It felt good to say it.

Mom is glaring at me, and I'm pretty sure she wants me to say sorry. In fact, I'm absolutely positive she wants me to say sorry. But I'm not sorry, and any kind of apology right now would be completely and totally ironic. I stay quiet.

When we get home, Savannah thanks Mom for the ride and gets out of the car without looking at me. But I catch a glimpse of a big, fat tear creeping out of the corner of her eye. I suddenly feel happy to see that tear, which I know is not right, but it's how I feel. As she walks away, I'm not sure if we are almost-always best friends or almost-never best friends or any kind of friends at all. And it's definitely weird.

Weird like a blobfish.

CHAPTER 13

We walk into the house after dropping Savannah off, and Mom wants to talk. I don't feel like talking. I feel like crawling into my bed and hiding under the covers for the rest of the summer. "We won't know anything until tomorrow," Mom reminds me again. But I don't need to wait until tomorrow. I saw the look on Mr. Sharp's face, and I know.

I sort of feel bad for Mom, because I can see that she's worried. But I'm afraid if I open my mouth at all, I'll start sobbing. I feel like a massive balloon of tears is pushed down inside me, trying to escape. And I'm working hard to not let it bob to the surface.

I'm not even sure what I'm the most upset about: *The Cat's Meow*, or Phoebe's dumb car commercial, or making Savannah cry, or how I left Jake hanging when he tried to high-five me on the way out of the studio. When we were six, Savannah and I could fight about things like who got to go on the monkey bars first and we'd figure it out in a nanosecond. No making up, no apologies necessary. When we were six, we could have invited Phoebe to play with us and I never once would have wondered whether I'd lose my best friend. When we were six, I played soccer with Jake at recess because it was fun, and didn't have to worry about what anyone else was thinking. Why can't we go back to taking turns, sharing our stuffed animals, and giggling around the mat at circle time? Why can't we go back to being six?

The smell of Dad's homemade meatballs cooking destroys my plan to stay in bed all summer long. They're my favorite, and Dad knows I can't resist them. I decide if I stick to "Yes, please" and "No, thank you" at dinner, I can make it through.

"Would you like some garlic bread?" Mom asks.

"Yes, please."

"Icy cold milk?" Dad asks.

"No, thank you."

It's working pretty well until Evan gets involved. I can tell he's trying to cheer me up.

"Do you wanna play Ocean Aliens after dinner?" he asks.

"No, thank you."

"But you can be the dolphin! You don't even have to be a space dolphin, you can be a real dolphin."

"No, thank you."

"Awww, Annie. You're so good at the dolphin noises and everything. Or you could be a mermaid— you can even sing the Ariel song if you want and I promise not to make throw-up faces while you do it, or zap you with my gamma ray during the performance, you're so good at—"

"STOP IT!" I yell. "STOP SAYING I'M GOOD AT THINGS! I'M NOT GOOD AT BEING A DOLPHIN, OR A MERMAID, OR A TV HOST, OR ANYTHING, EVER!" I jump out of my chair and race back to my room before I have to see the hurt look on Evan's face. As I run down the hallway, I feel the balloon inside me pop, and the tears start running down my cheeks. I crawl under my comforter and let them come.

Being under there with my sloppy tears gives me an idea for a great new product . . . a Kleenex dispenser that attaches to the inside of your bedspread.

But I'm so upset that I can't even come up with a script.

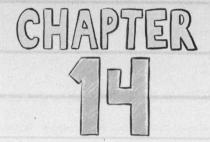

CHAPTER 14

"Wake up, Annie." It's Dad's voice, and he's gently shaking me.

I open my eyes, expecting it to still be dark outside, but it's not. It's morning.

"You slept for a long time!" he says. I snuggle up next to him, knowing that he wants to talk, and feeling like I might be able to.

"I'm sorry the audition didn't go the way you wanted it to," he begins.

"Yeah," I say.

"No matter what happens," he says, "Mom and I

are proud of you for going after something that you really wanted. When I was your age, I would have been too scared to even try. But you weren't, Annie, and I admire that. You've got pluck!"

"Did you wrinvent that word?" I ask.

"Nope," Dad says. "That's a gen-uuu-ine, find-it-in-the-dictionary, real-deal word. It means you've got courage, and you don't give up." I snuggle into his chest a little deeper. It is going to take all the pluck I've got to say what I want to say next.

"Sometimes," I begin slowly, "when a friend is good at something, I know I'm supposed to be happy, but I don't feel happy. I feel kind of sad and mad at the same time. And my head tries to tell my heart that I shouldn't be, but it's hard."

"It sure is," Dad says. "Feelings can be tough little guys, can't they?"

"Yep," I say.

"I feel that way sometimes, too. A writer friend will sell a story, while my stories sit on my computer, and I feel mad that it's not me selling a story, and sad that no one wants to read about Kikovin the elfin troll."

"So what do you do?" I ask.

"I let myself feel mad and sad for one day, and then I send them a card like this." He pulls a card out of the back pocket of his jeans. It has blue and yellow sparkly balloons all over it, and in giant red letters is the word CELEBRATE!

"So, sending the card is like your head telling your heart to be happy for your friend?" I ask.

"Exactly," Dad says.

I'm not sure I feel ready to celebrate with Savannah.

But I do feel ready to get out of this bed and find out what is going to happen with *The Cat's Meow*.

So I will get dressed and go back to that studio and look at the list.

Because I've got pluck.

CHAPTER 15

We're on our way back to the studio, and I'm trying not to worry about what will happen when we get there. I distract myself by writing a commercial for the Kleenex product I came up with last night.

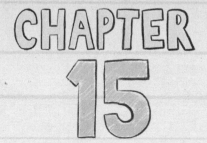

Life got you down? want to crawl inside your bed and have a good cry?

Everyone knows the best place to let those tears fall is right on your comfy pillow—but no one wants to blow their nose into a pillowcase! Yuck! Well, now you don't have to. Wipe those tears, because now there's the

TISSUE TUCK!

Attach it to the inside of your favorite blanket or comforter and you'll have tissues right there, right when you need them most. TISSUE TUCK comes in all your favorite colors and patterns, ready to cheer you up on your darkest days. Pink Leopard Print? We've got it. Ocean Turquoise? Of course! And we've even got an aliens theme for your little space enthusiast!

I reread the commercial and sigh. Pink leopard print is Savannah's favorite. Even when I'm trying not to think about her, I am thinking about her. I'm glad it's Saturday and her mom could drive her to the studio. I don't know what I would do if she was in the car right now.

Evan runs ahead to the door and swings it open for us. He bows and says in a stiff, robotic voice, "Enter, earthling!" I don't think he really understands exactly why I'm feeling the way I am, but he knows enough to be extra sweet to me, which is nice. We all walk inside. There are a few other kids milling around, but no Savannah. Raina-with-a-heart directs us to a sheet of paper held up on the wall with a bright green thumbtack. Dad grabs my hand on one side, and Mom grabs the other. Evan starts pretending to lasso Raina and put her on his spaceship. She looks uncomfortable, and it makes me giggle a little. I close my eyes and take a deep breath as we step toward the list. Mom and Dad squeeze my hands at almost the exact same time, and I open my eyes.

THE CAT'S MEOW!

HOST: SAVANNAH SUMMERLYN

There are other names on the list for smaller onscreen parts. One of them is Phoebe's, but none of them are mine. Last year, at the amusement park, I watched the Dastardly Dragon go around twelve times before I got in line to ride it. I knew the exact path of dips and turns and upside-downs that roller coaster would take. But even though I knew exactly what was going to happen, my stomach still dipped and dropped and got all churn-y. That's how I feel right now. Even though I knew I was going to see Savannah's name, I still think I might lose my corn dog.

"Okay," I say. Mom wraps her arm around my shoulder and gives me a side hug.

"Sorry, kiddo," she says.

Dad raises an eyebrow at me. "I'm thinking of writing a sequel to *Chippy the Poodlemunk*.

Whaddya think, want to help?" I know he's trying to get a smile out of me, so I give it to him. Evan runs over from Raina's desk and hands me a contraption made out of paper clips. "It's a UFO!" he says. "This one's for you, and then I'll build another one when we get home so we can do space races!" He pulls open his pocket to show us that he filled it with paper clips from Raina's desk.

I laugh, but Mom doesn't think it's funny. "Evan Edward Brown! Those aren't yours!" She drags Evan back over to Raina to return the paper clips. Dad and I are waiting for them to finish when Jake walks into the studio with his sister. "Well, Marathon Girl, what's the verdict? Are you in?"

My stomach drops again. It's one thing to see that your own name is not on the list. To know inside yourself that someone else won the thing you really wanted to win. And I've had a lot of practice with that, especially when it comes to being friends with Savannah. After you lose, you might feel different on the inside, but everything on the outside stays the same. You go to school and come home. You eat dinner and go to sleep, and pretty soon, you feel better and no one ever has to know how bad it felt.

Sometimes you can even try to remember things in a different way. Like the time I belly flopped so hard in Grammy's pool that I had a mark on my thigh from the impact of the water. I was all alone when it happened, and I cried. I never knew a belly flop could hurt so much! But when Mom asked about the red on my leg, I told her it was no big deal. And the more I said it, the more I remembered it that way. No tears, no pain, no big deal. But when someone is there to see you in the actual belly-flopping moment, you can't change it. The tears are there for them to see and remember. Part of you is super embarrassed that they saw it. But part of you is glad, because you'll never have to explain to that person why you're afraid of jumping into the pool like that again.

Jake is here, and he's smiling at me in his stupid soccer jersey, and my eyes start to fill up, and all I can think is that I don't want Jake to be the one who knows about my giant *Cat's Meow* belly flop. So I run away. I actually sprint to the bathroom. It's probably the fastest he's ever seen Marathon Girl run. I close the door and shut myself into the stall and wonder how long I can hide in here before someone comes in after me.

I guess I have the heart of a quail after all.

CHAPTER 16

If you've never run away to a public restroom from the boy who makes you feel barfy, then you might not know that the moment you flee is not the worst part. The worst part is when you are sitting on the toilet, well, not *actually* sitting on the toilet, but hiding in the stall, contemplating how to come out of the bathroom without seeming like a complete mess. And the problem with running away to the bathroom is that the obvious excuse is that you had to go to the bathroom. But telling an almost-sixth-grade boy you raced away from him because you *had to go*, well . . . that is not an option.

After two minutes of careful consideration, the only thing I can come up with that would fix the situation is a time machine. One that could take me even just five minutes earlier, so that I could act calm and collected when Jake showed up. Or maybe run somewhere other than the bathroom.

Do you constantly find yourself in embarrassing situations? Have you put your giant foot in your mouth once again? Wish you could turn back the clock and fix everything? Well, now, with our exclusive technology, you can!

ZIPPITY-ZOOM

You've read about time machines in your favorite sci-fi novels, but now, with our brand-new ZIPPITY-ZOOM, that dream is a reality! The ZIPPITY-ZOOM is the first of its kind.
Step inside, push a few buttons, and, in seconds, you'll be back to that mortifying moment.
Call or click now, supplies are limited!

What I should say is that supplies are nonexistent, since I'm pretty sure an actual time machine hasn't been invented yet. And the commercial needs some work. The phrase, "mortifying moment" sounds amazing when you say it out loud, especially in a TV announcer voice. But the thought of having to relive a mortifying moment? That doesn't actually sound too appealing.

The door squeaks open, and I hear a voice. Four minutes. I guess that's the answer to the question of how long I can hide in here.

"Annie?"

I sort of recognize the voice, but can't quite place it. I peek out through the sliver of light in the stall door and see a flash of pink. Phoebe. Okay, I take it back. . . . The worst part is when you are trying to figure out the best way to make your exit from the stall you're hiding in and the girl who you think might be trying to steal your almost-always best friend walks in.

I take a deep breath and open the door. While Phoebe being in here when I'm upset is bad, even worse would be Phoebe thinking that I've been using the bathroom for this long.

"Annie!" she says. "I'm so glad I found you! They're calling your name."

"My parents?" I say. "I'm pretty sure they saw me come in here."

"Not your parents, silly!" Phoebe squeals. "The producers! Jane is looking for you!"

Phoebe seems genuinely excited for me, and for an instant I think that maybe she's not so bad. But then I remember the "Ewwww," and kickball, and her hugging Savannah, and I change my mind.

"Thanks," I say, and walk past her to the door. But at the last second I turn around and say, "Orange." Phoebe looks confused, and I don't blame her. It's been four years, and who even remembers what their favorite color was in first grade? But there's something in me that needs to say it.

"Orange was my favorite color."

CHAPTER 17

Phoebe probably decides I'm completely cuckoo in the head, because she doesn't respond at all. We walk out, and Jake is waiting there with my family. He's teaching Evan to head a little Nerf soccer ball. I'm surprised my parents aren't telling them not to play ball inside, but I think they're just glad that Evan is busy and not trying to beam anyone into his UFO. "Heads up!" Jake calls out, tossing the soccer ball to me. I head the ball to the right of him, like he's the goalie and I'm trying to score off a corner kick. "Gooooooooooooooal!" he yells, and it makes me laugh.

No one says anything about my hundred-yard dash to the bathroom.

I hear my name again. "Annie?" I turn around and see Producer Jane poking her head out of the side door. "I'm so glad I caught you! Could you come in for a minute?" I look up at Mom and Dad with question marks in my eyes.

"Go ahead," Mom says. "We'll wait right here."

I walk through the door and my heart gasps a little when I see Mr. Sharp behind the table. I can't believe it, but today he is wearing a hat! His face is still awfully stern, but on his head is a plaid fedora, the kind of hat that my teacher, Mr. Lombardi, sometimes wore. I'm thinking this is a good sign.

"Annie," Mr. Sharp begins, "Jane and I have been talking about some help we are going to need with writing material for *The Cat's Meow*. We were impressed with the commercial you wrote for Fishlight, and would love to have a kid's perspective on our writing team. Do you have any other work for us to take a look at?"

I look down at the notebook in my hand. "I have another commercial," I say.

"Well then, let's take a look," he says. As he reads through the script for Tissue Tuck, I see the faintest smile appear on his face. It's only there for a moment, and then it's gone. But underneath that hat, I definitely saw his eyes get friendly for a second.

"Interesting," he says. "I think we can work with this."

"What Mr. Sharp means, Annie," Jane says with a smile, "is that we'd love to try you out as part of our writing team. Does that sound like something you'd like to do?"

"I wrote another commercial in the bathroom. I mean, not while I was *actually* in the bathroom, though I was in the stall . . ." I stop talking and start to wish that Savannah was here with me. She most definitely would give me the *REALLY*,

Annie?? look, but she would know the perfect thing to say. And everyone would laugh and relax, and not looked freaked out by the words that are coming out of my mouth. But she's not here, which means I'm on my own. I think about how professional Savannah sounded at the audition, and suddenly I know exactly what I should say.

"What I meant to say," I begin, "is that wrinventing is my passion. And I would love to be a part of *The Cat's Meow*."

I explain to them what it means to be a wrinventor, and though I still don't get a smile from Mr. Sharp, Jane does enough smiling for the both of them. And for the first time in what feels like forever, I don't want to be the opposite of Annie.

CHAPTER 18

I have writer's block. At the end of my time with
Jane and Mr. Sharp yesterday, they told me they
are considering creating a segment of *The Cat's
Meow* just for me. It would be called "Kids Think!"
and each week they would feature a product that
I come up with. So now I have to think of a few
different wrinventions for them to take a look at,
and if they work well in rehearsals, they'll make
the segment official and put them in the show. Jane
even said that at some point we might try making
prototypes of a few of the things I think up! Which

would be amazing, but I have to really impress them first. Problem is, suddenly I can't think of anything.

Jane also asked me to come up with a tagline for Savannah. A tagline is something the on-air personality says at the end of every show. It has to be completely original and so creative that when people hear it, they automatically say, "Oh, that's Savannah Summerlyn!" Jane told me that she thought I would be the perfect person to write the tagline since Savannah and I are best friends. I didn't mention to her the fact that we are not even speaking to each other right now. I didn't think that would be very professional.

Nothing is coming to me, so it's time for a break. I walk into the kitchen and grab a piece of watermelon from the bowl on the table. I bite into it, and, as the sticky juice starts to run down my hands, the perfect idea hits me.

Love watermelon, but don't love the mess it makes? Backyard picnic ruined by sticky fingers? Tired of picking up a healthy piece of fruit, only to want to put it right back down again? Stop. There's a better way!

Introducing

melon mitts

the washable gloves you put on right before you bite into that delicious summer treat.

Not bad. I was starting to worry, because my dad sometimes has writer's block that lasts a couple of weeks. And since I have his passion for writing, I was scared that maybe writer's block was genetic, too. One time, when Dad's writer's block was especially bad, he told me his muse was on vacation, and asked if I would help him interview for a replacement. Before that, I didn't even know what a muse was, but Dad explained that it was this sort of pretend person that an artist thinks of as their inspiration. It was pretty fun coming up with interview questions for his imaginary candidates. My favorite was a merman named Herman, who wanted to be an opera singer. He was a keeper. Some people might find it weird, talking to imaginary people with their dad. But we writers know that it's part of the creative process.

For now, the Melon Mitts commercial is a keeper, too. I'm washing the watermelon juice off my hands at the sink when I see Savannah next door in her driveway. I feel a pang in my chest, like when you're thinking about doing something that makes you feel excited and scared at the same time. Like the first time I climbed to the top of the rock wall at the school carnival. This *Cat's Meow* thing is big, and this is the only time in five years that I've gone more than a day without talking to Savannah. Even when my family went camping last summer, we talked on the phone. I think about that *Good friends are like stars* poster on her wall, and it seems a little less creepy. Maybe almost-always best friends are like stars. Savannah could still be there in the sky. All I need to do is wait for the clouds to pass over so that I can see her again.

I usually run most of my commercials by Savannah. She almost always loves them. The only one she ever vetoed was Cat Crunchers, since they were 3-D cat-shaped crackers, and she felt they promoted violence against cats. I'm pretty sure she would love the idea of Melon Mitts, since watermelon is her favorite fruit, and she absolutely hates getting messy. I glance out the window again and she's sitting down now on the driveway, like she's waiting for something.

Or someone.

Of course! Savannah has been in this very spot in our kitchen a bazillion times. She knows this window looks out to her driveway. This is clearly her way of telling me she wants to talk to me.

I finish drying my hands on my pants and quick-jog to the front door. "Be right back!" I yell behind me. Not sure if my parents are even paying attention, but once Savannah and I start talking again, I may be gone for a while, and I don't want them to worry about where I went. We have *a lot* to catch up on. I start across the grass, making my way toward her. "Hey, Sav—" I begin, but my words are cut off by the sound of tires crunching on her gravelly driveway. A car I don't recognize pulls in. The door opens, and out pops Phoebe. Even the way she gets out of a car is overly perky.

I'm not sure if Savannah saw me or not, but Phoebe definitely hasn't seen me, and I don't want her to. Out of the corner of my eye, I spy our trash cans, still at the curb from the garbage pickup this morning. I sprint over and crouch down behind them as Phoebe runs up the driveway and hugs Savannah. *Hugs* her. Again. What is with Phoebe and the hugging? Hugging is for when your aunt Roberta comes to visit once a year. Not for people you see all the time. But Savannah doesn't seem to mind. Is it possible that all this time the one thing Savannah wished for in a best friend is that they would be a hugger?

Phoebe's head swings around in my direction, and I scooch closer to a trash can. Something brown and mushy is dripping down the side, and the smell makes my stomach lurch. It's probably just the remains of last night's beef stroganoff, but I do wish they would hurry up and go inside so I can get out of here. The crouching is making my right foot all pins-and-needles-y, so I shift my weight to the left. Finally, more tire crunching tells me Phoebe's parents' car is pulling away, and I peek around the side of the trash can to make sure the coast is clear. But when I do, I see Phoebe and Savannah walking right toward me. Even worse, Phoebe looks me square in the eyeball, and I know for certain that the coast is most definitely not clear.

"I knew I heard something over here!" Phoebe says in a way-too-loud voice. "I was guessing it was that mangy old cat from down the street. But look, it's Annie!" Ugh. Phoebe is really good at saying things that seem normal and nice, but feel like an insult.

There's no escaping them at this point, so I try to stand up from behind the garbage. But my right foot, which has now gone completely numb, can't support my weight. I put my hand out to steady myself on the trash can, but lose my balance. I tumble backward, pulling last night's leftovers on top of me.

Yup, beef stroganoff.

"Annie?" Savannah rushes over, but I'm too quick. I've got the can right-side up and am flicking noodles off my pants before she gets there.

"Just working on a new product idea for the show!" I say. "Waterproof jumpsuits for garbage collectors! Made from bacteria-resistant materials!" Wow, so much for writer's block. That's a pretty good idea. I don't know where it's coming from, but the loud, loud words keep rolling out. "They'll be called RUBBISH RAGS! Or GARBAGE GARB! Or maybe, I don't know . . . WASTE WEAR!"

Savannah has this confused look on her face, like the one she gives Old Man Miller when he lines his pickle jars up on his front porch. Mr. Miller lives down the street from us, and he's always doing strange stuff. One time he was clipping his toenails into a coffee mug as we walked by, and then later that same day we saw him drinking his coffee right out of the same mug. Some people might think that's funny, but we didn't. We both agreed that it was the saddest thing we had ever seen. And that's how Savannah is looking at me right now. Like she's just seen me slurp up a huge mug full of toenails. Like she feels sorry for me. Like she doesn't know me at all.

Before either one of them can say anything more, I put the lid back on the can and wave good-bye. "Well, I guess I'll see you later," I say, and hustle back to the house.

From the window, I watch them walk away, into Savannah's house. They are both wearing pink, and it makes me realize that Phoebe and Savannah are a lot alike. That all the enthusiasm and energy that I love most about Savannah is the same stuff that bugs me about Phoebe. And now I'm thinking that maybe the one in this whole picture that doesn't belong is me. Phoebe is the one who's heading into Savannah's house to hang out in her room. Savannah will make Phoebe laugh by calling her mom "Lynda," and they'll eat graham crackers with peanut butter. Savannah will tell Phoebe the story about the hole in her dollhouse, and they'll laugh some more. At me.

As I hop in the shower to clean off the vat of stink, I wonder if the perfect tagline for Savannah is simple. "This is Savannah Summerlyn for *The Cat's Meow.* . . . Good-bye."

CHAPTER 19

After dinner, Mom suggests a walk to the park. Even though she hasn't said anything about it, I know that she's noticed Savannah hasn't been around the last few days. I can tell she's concerned because she's been checking on me a lot—rubbing my back and smoothing my hair, and asking all sorts of questions. Like if I'm cold, or if I'm feeling tired, or need a snack. It's funny because I feel like she asks every question except the one question she really wants to ask, which is "What is going on with you and Savannah?" Part of me wants her to ask, because then I could tell her how miserable and confused I am. But the other part of me appreciates her not asking, because it is a question that I don't have the answer to.

So when Mom suggests going to the park for some "soccer therapy," we all put on our shoes and head out the door. The park is about eight blocks from our house. The walk feels easy on the way there, but the park is just far away enough that when it's time to go home, I always wish we had brought the car.

I decide our walk is the perfect time to take up my campaign, once again, for a dog. I'm always telling them that our walks to the park would be made more perfect by the presence of a yellow Labrador retriever named Goldie.

"What a lovely night for a stroll," I say. Mom loves it when we sing the praises of walking. I'm big-time trying to butter her up.

"Seriously, could it get any better than this?" she says.

"Well, in the Land of Triumph, it's always a perfect seventy-five degrees. The woodland creatures can't survive unless their environment is controlled precisely. Well, they could survive, but their magic couldn't," Dad chimes in.

"Daaaaaaaaaaad!" I groan.

"So I'd say," he says as he checks the weather on his phone, "that it's eleven degrees too warm out here, that is, if you ever expect to defeat King Kalliope, Ruler of the Ogres and Destroyer of all that is good and righteous!" As he talks about the evil ogre, he throws his arms out in front of him like Frankenstein and starts to chase me. I let myself be caught, and he picks me up and tickles me.

"Did you know," Evan starts, "that some alien life forms can survive in extreme temperatures? They could literally live inside a freezer, or a pot of boiling water!"

"Or inside a snowman!" Mom says.

"Or a spaghetti dinner!" Dad says.

"Or a bowl of ice cream!" Evan says.

"Or a chocolate lava cake!" I join in.

And I completely forget about my mission to convince my parents to get a dog, and I just laugh. I don't know if it's the magic of woodland creatures, or miraculous Zippity-Zoom time travel, or the plain old comfort of being with people who love you most (even when you're not a hugger), but I catch up to Mom and grab her hand. We let our joined hands swing big between us, and it's like I'm six again.

When we arrive at the park, Mom and Dad head over to the playground with Evan, while I practice juggling with the soccer ball we brought. Juggling in soccer is not the same as regular juggling, since there's only one ball and you use your feet instead of your hands. I'm not very good at it, which is why I need to practice. The park is pretty crowded, so I don't even see Jake until he is standing right next to me. He tries to steal the soccer ball, but I do a quick reverse step over and keep possession. He goes after the ball again, but I have quick feet. It's only when I have to use my left foot to avoid dribbling into a baby stroller that I lose the ball to him.

Jake picks up the ball while the stroller goes by. "So, are you doing okay?" he asks.

I'm pretty sure he's talking about *The Cat's Meow*, but I decide to pretend that I don't know that.

"Other than not having a left foot, I'm doing fine," I say.

Jake laughs and sends the ball back to me. "Riley didn't get the part she wanted for the web-show thingy, either."

For a minute, I had totally forgotten that his sister had tried out. "Oh, that's right. Was she bummed?"

"Yeah, especially that someone younger than her got the role. She thought an eighth grader should get it."

"Wow," I say. I think about Savannah beating out an eighth grader, and I feel proud. Not a barfy-disappointed kind of proud. A real-deal, gen-uuuu-ine kind of proud.

"You would have been good . . . you know . . . as the host? I thought you would get it." Jake looks the tiniest bit embarrassed as he says it, and this time, I'm the one smiling.

"Thanks," I say. "I might still be a part of it, actually. They liked the writing I did for my audition and asked me to do some more."

"Writing?" Jake says. "Like what kind of writing?"

I never thought in a million years I would be telling Jake about my wrinventing but he's here and he's asking questions like he's interested in my crazy hobby, like he's interested in the things I write about, like he's interested in . . . me. So I tell him.

"Oh!" Jake says. "Like the presentation you did for U.S. History? The plaid shirts with parts of the Consti-tution sewn into them? What were they called again?"

"Freedom Flannels!" I say, surprised he remembers.

"Yes!" Jake says. "That was so funny. Do you remember any of it?"

I hesitate a little, not sure I'm performance-ready. But Jake is so enthusiastic I can't say no. I march in place and launch into the part I can remember.

"Coming to you live from Philadelphia, the Founding Fathers present . . . FREEDOM FLAN-NELS! Can't remember more than 'We the People'? Get confused about which amendment is which? Well, guess no more with FREEDOM FLANNELS, the shirt that won't let you forget your rights! We didn't sail all the way from Britain to go back to our old ways. Let a FREEDOM FLANNEL protect you from the cold and from religious persecution!"

I march around some more and pretend to play a flute, and Jake cracks up.

"How do you come up with this stuff?" he asks.

I shrug and play it cool but am secretly pretty happy that he's impressed.

"You know, I might be doing something for *The Cat's Meow*, too," Jake says.

"Really?" I ask. What is he talking about?

"I wasn't planning to try out for it, but when I was there, waiting for Riley, the lady with the pink hair asked about the soccer jersey I was wearing. We talked about soccer and the next thing I knew, I was standing in front of the cranky dude, demonstrating a double scissor move."

"That's awesome!" I say. I feel kind of bad that I didn't even know that Jake was going to be on the show. I've been way too wrapped up in my own drama. "Better get back to practicing then!" I say as I pass the ball back to him again. I think of the *Good friends are like stars* poster and wonder if maybe it got something wrong, because stars are millions of miles away in the sky. And while I'm not sure whether or not Jake and I are good friends, I've definitely been a million miles away. Can you really be a good friend to someone when you are so far away that you don't even ask them how they are doing?

We keep passing the ball back and forth until Mom and Dad and Evan come back from the playground. It's starting to get dark, but we all make a circle and play keep-away with our feet. When it's my turn in the mush pot, Jake launches the ball into the air, and instead of trying to trap it, I catch it.

"Hey, no hands!" Mom calls out.

But I run wild away from them, and everyone starts to laugh. I keep running into the sunset with the ball in my arms, not caring if it's against the rules, or if it means I lost the game. Because I'm not keeping score.

CHAPTER 20

It's hard to believe that it's been so long since I talked to Savannah. But there's no getting around it today; the entire cast and crew is meeting up at *The Cat's Meow*. I will have to face her. Her and the poofy pink hug monster. I should probably thank Phoebe because worrying about her helped me come up with another great product idea for Kids Think! It's a company that builds stuffed monsters based on your personality.

Parents, tired of kids who come into your room at night, scared of the boogeyman? Kids, would you sleep better knowing that creepy creature in your room is actually a friend? Well, guess what? Monsters aren't just for under the bed anymore! At

CUSTOM CREATURES

we build a special monster just for you! Love singing and dancing? Try Gladys Glee, our top-selling critter that croons. See space travel in your future? We'll send you Archie Astro, a bodacious beast who loves the stars! Tell us what you're all about, and we'll make you your own personal monster and send it out!

I designed Gladys Glee especially for Savannah. I've thought it through and decided that when I see her today, I will forgive her. She is my almost-always best friend, after all. And while we've been caught in the "almost" part for a few days now, I'd really like to get back to the "best friend" part. I worked it all out in my head. When I arrive at the set of *The Cat's Meow*, she will see me and all of those best friend fuzzies will come rushing back. She'll drop everything (including Phoebe) to run to me and beg for forgiveness. She might even try to get down on her knees. But I won't allow her to, because best friends don't let best friends get the knees of their favorite jeans dirty. Unless there was some sort of protective covers you could put over them, like kneepads, but not the kind you wear for volleyball. They'd have to be cute. Wait! That's a really good idea!

Have you said something you didn't mean? Snatched your best friend's dreams away from her once again? Do you find yourself having to get down on your knees and beg for her to take you back?

Introducing

Apology Armor,

the kneepads you wear on the days you have to say sorry.

APOLOGY ARMOR is available in colors and patterns to match every outfit. Purple plaid for the days you're feeling bookish. Orange and yellow polka dots for the days you're feeling sunny. And our world-famous Glitter Gala pads will blend in with the fanciest of outfits.

Don't hesitate. Order now and we'll throw in a second pair of APOLOGY ARMOR for only ninety-nine cents!

Even without Apology Armor, I'm absolutely positive that Savannah will apologize today. I'll say, "I'm glad to see you've come to your senses. I forgive you." And then Savannah will link her arm in mine, and we'll both forget that Phoebe ever existed. It's a perfect plan. And in it, I've given Savannah the most dramatic role, which suits her.

When I worked it out in my head, I tried it the other way around, too. Where I am the one who apologizes. But what would I say? "I'm sorry you stole my audition"? I mean, that would be a 100 percent true statement, with not one little bit of irony involved. I'm sorry the whole thing happened at all. But if I jumped into my Zippity-Zoom and went back to the audition, what would I change? I was nervous, yes, but being nervous is hardly a crime. She was the one who was charming and bouncy and absolutely delightful. She is definitely the one who needs to apologize.

I've written the script a few different ways. They all start with her racing over to me when I walk through the door and end with her being sorry for everything, including all the Phoebe business.

You were right all along, Annie! I'm so sorry for being such a terrible friend. And I'm especially sorry for wearing pink and hanging out with Phoebe.

Or *Annie, you are the best friend a girl could ask for. I don't need Phoebe, and I'm sorry for everything that has happened in the last few days. Especially all the hugging.*

Or The Cat's Meow *means nothing to me! Phoebe means nothing to me! The only thing in the whole wide world that means anything to me is your friendship! Please take me back!*

This is where Savannah throws herself on the ground and refuses to get back up until I agree to forgive her. Apology Armor would be super helpful. Maybe I can transform my brother's skateboarding pads into something workable. I get out my sketchpad and start designing a prototype.

"Annie! Time to go! Gotta get my little writer to

her first gig!" Dad calls down the hall. I'm not sure who's more excited about me writing for *The Cat's Meow*, me or Dad. I throw down my sketches and bounce to the front door, excited to get to the studio. My apology awaits. Today is the day I get my best friend back.

CHAPTER 21

I worked really hard to come up with a tagline for Savannah. I did some research on the most famous news anchors in history and how they signed off on their shows. And every single one of them said something so simple and ordinary, but somehow it became their signature line. Edward R. Murrow said, "Good night, and good luck." Walter Cronkite said, "And that's the way it is." I can't figure out if they actually meant to be that uninteresting, or if they couldn't help it because it was back in the old days when things seemed to be more boring in general. I did notice in my research that there weren't any women on the news back then. So that could have been the problem. I am determined to make Savannah's tagline better than those old-timey ones. Which, frankly, hasn't been that difficult. I came up with a few different options:

This is Savannah Summerlyn, whirling and twirling away until next time on The Cat's Meow.

Savannah Summerlyn, singing off until next time on The Cat's Meow*!* (Instead of signing off, she would be "singing" off—she could actually sing it, too!)

But my favorite one is: *This has been Savannah Summerlyn for* The Cat's Meow. *Until next time, shine on like the star you are!* "Shine on like the star you are" isn't something I would say in a zillion years. But that's the thing I'm learning about writing for someone else. You have to write it the way that person would say it. And that's definitely something Savannah would say. Plus, every time I look at it on the page, I think of her poster about friends and stars and feel hopeful.

"Well, Miss Annie-Pants, how are you feeling about your big writing debut?" Dad asks as we drive to the studio.

"I'd feel a lot better if you didn't call me Annie-Pants," I say.

"Oh, I'm sorry, do you prefer Annie-*Pantalones*?" He says this with his best Spanish accent, which is sort of terrible, and I can't help but laugh. He pulls the car into a parking spot in front of the studio and I hop out. *"Adios, señor!"* I call out and swing the door shut.

I walk into the studio and see Savannah right away. She's standing alone, and, for once, *she* looks kind of nervous. She's wearing a fuzzy purple sweater that must be new because I've never seen it before. But I'm not surprised to see her wearing purple, because she calls it her "happy color." I try to catch her eye, but she's staring off in the other direction, so I decide to go over to her. It's not how I planned it, since she was supposed to see me first, drop everything, and run over, but that seems like such a little thing now that I'm here and she's there, and she doesn't have anything to drop anyway.

I'm about halfway there when she gets this huge smile on her face. I'm thinking that maybe she saw me coming. I never saw her eyes turn in my direction, but she must have seen me when I looked down at my shoes for a split second. As I almost reach her, she squeals and throws her arms out in front of her, and I think that maybe this one time I will go ahead and hug her. Except she's still facing the wrong direction. I'm thinking that's okay, I'll just change my path a bit and hug her anyway, but then I realize that she's already hugging someone. Someone wearing an awful lot of pink. Someone who's definitely not me. It's too late to change direction, and next thing you know I practically fall right into the lovefest in front of me. My almost-always best friend and the bubblegum queen.

"Hi, Annie!" Phoebe squeals, too, and tries to pull me into the bouncing-hugging-squealing circle of doom. I squirm my way out of her grasp and manage to narrowly escape. "Don't you simply adore Savannah's new sweater? It is *beyond* cute, isn't it? We found it yesterday in the clearance bin! Can you believe it? It brings out her eyes, makes them look almost violet. It's going to absolutely pop on camera!"

And I'm sure Phoebe is thinking once again that I'm completely cuckoo because I'm standing there in silence, staring at them. This isn't at all what I planned, and now I don't know how the rest of the script reads. I try to focus only on Savannah and, amazingly, it works. I take a deep breath, look her in the eye, and am about to ask for my apology when Phoebe opens her big mouth again and says, "Oh, and congratulations, Annie! I was so excited when I heard they found a place for your silly little commercials!"

Silly?

Little?

At that moment, my face turns the most intense shade of red. Really red. The Hue Guru would probably call it Screaming Scarlet. Or Apple Anger. Or Firework Fury. I wait a minute, sure that Savannah is going to say something. That she'll defend me, my commercials, my passion. But she just looks at me. And now I'm thinking that maybe I was wrong. That maybe today is not the day I get my best friend back. In fact, it might be the day that I lose her forever.

CHAPTER 22

"Okay, listen up, everyone!" Jane calls us all over to her. My mouth is still hanging open from Phoebe's comment, but I have no choice but to ignore it and gather around Jane. "We are all so excited to be here together today! Today is like one big practice. We're going to get to know one another and how things work, so that when we are ready to film, we'll be prepared." She sends Savannah and the other on-air kids over to Mr. Sharp, and pulls me aside.

Jane asks to see what I've written, so I hand her my notebook. She vetoes the singing tagline, but likes the other two. "We'll try these out on camera today and see what feels right for Savannah," she says. "Good work!" She's also a big fan of the Custom Creatures commercial. I think about suggesting that we dress Phoebe up as a monster so that the viewers would really get a feel for the product. But I stop myself, because I don't think that would be very professional.

Mr. Sharp is still prepping Savannah and the other kids, so I sit in the corner and wait. I am in shock that Savannah didn't say anything to Phoebe. She knows how much my commercials mean to me and I would never, not in a zillion years, let someone call her passion silly. Or little. I look again at the taglines I wrote for her and they suddenly seem all wrong.

This is Savannah Summerlyn, whirling and twirling away until next time on The Cat's Meow.

This has been Savannah Summerlyn for The Cat's Meow. *Until next time, shine on like the star you are!*

I turn to a fresh page and rewrite them.

Savannah's Taglines, Take 2:

This is Savannah Summerlyn, driving friends away until next time on The Cat's Meow.

This has been Savannah Summerlyn for The Cat's Meow. *Until next time, shine on like the star you are, but I'm definitely not!*

I read them again and know that they're awful and mean. But see, this is why I like writing. Because I can write down all of my feelings, get them all out on paper, and no one ever has to see them but me. Who knows—if I didn't have writing, I might let these feelings out into the world. I might say them to people, and that would be truly awful.

"Okay, people, let's do this!" Mr. Sharp is ready to roll. The words he says are harmless, but his voice is prickly, like he's teetering on the edge of cranky canyon. I'm starting to wonder if maybe he's one of those people who enjoys acting upset all the time. He's got Savannah set up in front of the camera. She has to be sure to stay on this little spot they keep calling her "mark." Guess there won't be a lot of whirling and twirling today.

"Where's her script? Jaaaaane?" He's sort of bellowing now, and even Jane looks a little freaked out.

"Um, it seems to be misplaced at the moment," she says. Raina, who was introduced to us this morning as Jane's assistant, looks frantic, and Jane's doing this sort of quick-jog thingy over to Mr. Sharp while she tries to explain herself.

"I hope this isn't an indication of how the rest of this day is going to go." Mr. Sharp sure is living up to his name, as everything that comes out of his mouth right now seems to sting. Even the adults in the room flinch a little every time he opens it. I look around and see that Phoebe's eyes are huge. She looks a little like Red Riding Hood staring right into the mouth of the Big Bad Wolf. Phoebe might be scared, but I'm not. I saw the softer side of Mr. Sharp when he read my writing and wore that hat. If I try super hard, I can even pretend that he's my teacher, Mr. Lombardi, and Mr. Lombardi doesn't even kill the spiders in his own house. He told us that he catches them and takes them outside "to live the life they were meant to." True story. So I think, *Mr. Lombardi, Mr. Lombardi, Mr. Lombardi* . . . and go for it.

"Um . . . Mr. Lom . . . I mean, Mr. Sharp?" My words ring out through the paper shuffling and murmuring, and then it's silent.

"Yes?" he replies. He still sounds a touch annoyed, but I've come this far and I'm not going to let it stop me.

"Maybe, while we look for the script, this would be a good time to try out the taglines I wrote for Savannah?"

He pauses and kind of looks me up and down, and I'm wondering if he even remembers my name. Finally, he speaks. "Now that's what I like to see, a young person with a little initiative! Absolutely. Let these ninnies try to figure out where the script is, and in the meantime, we'll be productive. Let's get started, shall we?"

I hand my notebook to Raina, and she races it over to Savannah. I'm beaming, so proud of myself for speaking up, especially to someone like Mr. Sharp. And he called me a young person with "initiative"! I'll have to ask Dad about that word on the way home, but I could tell from the way he said it that it was a good thing. I look up and see that Savannah is smiling at me, too. She looks proud. Not a barfy-disappointed kind of proud, either. A real-deal, genuine kind of proud.

I start to think that everything is going to be okay, that Savannah and I can go back to being macaroni and cheese, and Phoebe wouldn't even be so terrible as, like, a side of broccoli, when I realize something very, very bad.

When I was Screaming Scarlet and Firework Fury, I wrote some not-so-nice things in that notebook. The notebook that is now being handed to Savannah. And I never turned the page.

CHAPTER

23

I'm scrambling for a fix to this completely disastrous problem, but it's like my brain waves are on fast-forward and I can't slow them down. Like that time the cursor on Dad's laptop got stuck in the scrolling position. Everything kept moving down, down, down until it got to the bottom. We would watch it get to the end and think it was finally over, but then it would jump back up to the top and start all over again. Constant motion. And it was moving so fast you couldn't ever get your eyes to really see anything. The only way we were able to fix it was to reboot the computer. Shut it down completely and begin again. I wish this day had a reboot button.

Savannah's eyes are glued to the notebook, and I know she's read what I wrote. I see the tears forming in her eyes and my stomach drops, and now I'm barfy disappointed, without the tiniest trace of happy. I'm barfy disappointed . . . in me.

"Okay, Savannah. I'd like to get you on camera running these lines, so make sure you look right over here as you say them. And don't forget that smile!" Mr. Sharp gives Savannah her instructions, and she finally lifts her head from the page. Her eyes find mine, and I send her the biggest *I'm so, so sorry* look I can muster. I want to be able to see *It's okay*, or *I forgive you*, or *Good friends are like stars* in her eyes as she stares back at me, but all I can see is hurt. And it's awful.

It occurs to me that Savannah has my future at *The Cat's Meow* in her hands. If she reads those lines out loud, my Kids Think! segment will never happen. Those lines I wrote are anything but professional. Yep, if Savannah reads those taglines, I'm done. Mr. Sharp raps his pen on his clipboard. "What's the holdup, Ms. Summerlyn?"

Savannah is frozen in place. There is a long silence. Too long. Like a hundred-degrees-outside-so-hot-you-want-to-cry-waiting-for-the-car-AC-to-kick-in kind of loooooong. And this is the part where, if I were Savannah, I would know the exact right thing to say or do, to rescue her. But I'm not Savannah. I keep waiting for her to read the lines. To read the awfulness that I wrote and seal my fate.

But she doesn't.

"Um." Savannah's voice comes out so soft, a voice that is so completely un-Savannah, I'm not sure Mr. Sharp can hear her. "Could we, um, take five?"

Mr. Sharp looks like he's holding his breath. I wonder if he's doing one of those anger management exercises, where they have you count to ten before you say something you'll regret. I'm starting to wonder who thought that Mr. Sharp working with kids would be a good idea.

Jane swoops in and puts an arm around Savannah. "Yes, let's take five . . . and this is a great opportunity to say to everyone that stage fright is totally normal, and it's okay to stop and take a breath if you need to." She guides Savannah to the other side of the room, where Phoebe takes over. I watch Phoebe whispering and rubbing Savannah's arm, and while it makes my insides flip-flop, I think that I deserve this. I deserve to be stuck in the corner of the room by myself, watching someone else be a great friend to Savannah. And, for the first time since this whole thing started, I'm sorry. I'm sorry for trying to take Savannah's Heart of a Quail Award, and for putting a hole in the roof of her dollhouse. I'm sorry for yelling at her in the car after the audition, and for wishing she would be a disappearing star. But most of all, I'm sorry for thinking that Savannah was not a good friend, because I'm pretty sure that in this moment, the one who is being an almost-never best friend is me.

Everyone in this room thinks Savannah has stage fright, and it's my fault. I run over to Raina, who is carrying my notebook around with her. "Just a quick edit," I say, as I take the notebook back. I rip out the page that says *Savannah Taglines: Take 2*, and turn it to the correct page, right as Mr. Sharp calls everyone back. Raina hands the notebook back to Savannah, and I rip the page in my hand into a zillion tiny pieces.

Savannah returns to her mark and reads the lines. The right ones. And they're great. They're great because Savannah reads them with expression and enthusiasm. They're great because there's something about my writing and her reading that is perfect together. They're great, like we used to be.

CHAPTER 24

We only meet on Tuesdays and Thursdays for *The Cat's Meow* and today is Wednesday, so I get the day to wrinvent. Tomorrow is the day that they will make a decision about whether or not they're going to include the Kids Think! segment, and they want me to run one of my wrinventions on camera. *On camera!* I'm sitting at the kitchen table, trying to come up with some more ideas, but instead I keep wondering about this alien-like creature called an African lungfish that Evan told us about at dinner last night. (Don't get me started on Evan talking about gross things at dinner; it's something that happens way too often. And, trust me, trying to eat noodle casserole while listening to him describe the digestive tract of a deep-sea tubeworm is not easy.)

He was telling us about it because the African lungfish is an example of how life-forms—like aliens—can adapt to their environments, no matter how extreme. African lungfish normally like to live in shallow pools of water. But sometimes those water pools dry up. Most fish would die without the water, but the African lungfish burrows itself deep into the mud and forms a cocoon around itself. We won't talk about the fact that this cocoon is made of mucus. Except I just did, so . . . yuck. But in the mud and mucus, this fish can continue to live, even though it has no water.

The whole time Evan was describing this gruesome scene, I kept wanting to ask him: Was the African lungfish happy? Because splashing around in a pool of water with your other lungfish friends sounds like a great life. But when this difficult thing happens, and the water disappears, they have no choice but to sink down into the mud and mucus, alone. It's this totally amazing thing that they can survive, but what kind of life is that, alone and in the mud?

Yesterday, while *The Cat's Meow* rehearsal was finishing up, I thought through a bunch of different ways I could apologize to Savannah. I could bring her a huge bouquet of tulips with a funny joke attached. *(What flower grows on faces? Two-lips!)* I could put my hair back in the send-up-a-flare hot-pink bow and do the *Tabitha* dance for her. I could put on some Apology Armor, get down on my knees, and refuse to get up until she takes me back. Whatever I do, it has to be good. Simply saying sorry doesn't feel like enough.

Making Savannah laugh is an absolutely necessary part of this apology. Right now when I think about her all I can see is that awful *How could you?* look she had on her face after she read those taglines. It is my mission to erase that picture from my memory for life. She left the studio yesterday hand-in-hand with Phoebe. She didn't even look at me. I have to make things better.

Because if I don't, then I'll be the one that ends up like that African lungfish. Savannah gets to swim off into clearer waters with Phoebe. But I'm alone in the mud and a cocoon of yuck. I'm pretty sure I could survive—the last few days without Savannah have proved it. But who wants to live like that?

Just as I'm imagining myself sinking, sinking, sinking down into the muck, doomed to life as the loneliest lungfish, there's a knock on our door. I open it and Jake is standing there, shuffling some papers around in his hands.

"Hey, MG," he says.

"Hey," I say back. We stand there, and it's quiet and awkward, and I'm thinking that boys are so weird because it seems like all they ever say is "hey," like that one little word somehow communicates everything. If Savannah were at the door right now, she would have told me three times over exactly why she was there. "So . . . ," I start, hoping that will spark something for Jake, something that will remind him that there might be a reason he showed up on my doorstep.

"Yeah, so, um . . . I'm trying to work on this soccer thing for *The Cat's Meow* and it turns out that I am terrible at coming up with ideas. Doing the soccer moves is no problem, but actually knowing what I'm going to say while I do them is impossible." Jake always seems so confident with his goofy smile and the way he lets stupid teasing bounce right off of him, so it's a little odd to see him like this—like he's nervous or something.

He keeps going, "I have to write like an intro thing for myself and then a script that explains each part of the move. Since you know so much about soccer, and I know how much you like to write, I was hoping you could maybe help me?"

Right then I hear Dad behind me, swinging the door all the way open. "You've come to the right place, Jacob! Come on in to Annie's writing cave. Of course, there will be a small fee for her editing services . . . a dozen or two of your family's famous tamales should do the trick!"

Jake laughs, and I roll my eyes. We head to the kitchen table and get to work. I convince him to come up with a catchy name for his segment.

Welcome to Mastering Moves with Jake Ramirez! Sharpen your shots, polish your passing, and strengthen that step over with the finest forward in fútbol!

I make Jake practice it, and he keeps stumbling over the "finest forward in fútbol" part. At first, it seems like it's because there are too many *f*'s and it's too tongue-twister-y. But when I offer to revise it, Jake hesitates.

"It's not that it's hard to say the words," he begins. "It's more that it feels weird to call myself the finest forward in futbol, when it's not actually true. There are lots of kids who score more goals than me."

"But," I argue, "you set up lots of shots. Your role is just as important, even if it sometimes feels . . . invisible."

Jake nods and looks at me like he's trying to figure something out. And then he's smiling again, but it's a different kind of smile this time, like he knows something that I don't. Right as I'm thinking I might have to get up from this table and flee like a quail again, he says, "I guess we have a lot in common."

"We do?"

"Yeah, I mean, being good at the job that no one really sees. You might not be the one that everyone gets excited about, but without you, it would have never happened."

I don't know if Jake is talking about soccer, or writing, or just life in general. But his words sink in and the blurry edges of my mind snap into focus. It's like that time we drove to the coast and there was so much fog that Mom could barely see the car in front of her. It was scary, and I wanted to pull over. But as we continued to drive, the wind kicked up and blew the fog away from us. One minute we were driving in soup, and the next we could see for miles. Jake's words are like that breeze, pushing away the confusion, clearing the road so I can see.

"Like a troubadour," I say.

"Like a what?" Jake asks.

Where do I even start? How do I talk about this strange word that in the last couple of weeks has become part of my everyday vocabulary? I'm looking at Jake, right in his ginormous brown eyes, trying to decide whether to explain, when he crosses them and pushes his nose up with his index finger.

I sigh and roll my eyes. Maybe another time.

"Now don't forget," Jake says, getting up from the table, "that invisibility can come in extremely handy. You know, for getting away with stuff."

"Okay, Harry Potter. I'll remember that the next time I'm hatching a dragon egg."

Jake laughs and grabs his papers. "Thanks for helping me. You are an amazing writer." I walk him to the door, and, before stepping out, he turns around and puts his hand up for a high five. I throw my hand against his, but this time, for the briefest second, he squeezes my hand before dropping it.

"See ya, Marathon Girl."

"See ya."

Somewhere in between writing Jake's intro, trying to understand the barfy feeling I have in my stomach when he calls me "an amazing writer," and that hand squeeze, I've come up with the perfect way to fix things with Savannah. I open my notebook and start writing. This has to work.

CHAPTER 25

"Hey!" I hear Jake's voice before I see him, and I'm surprised. I just arrived at the studio for our Thursday rehearsal, and I was so focused on going over this Savannah thing in my head that I didn't even see him. They should put a picture of Jake on that *Good friends are like stars* poster. Because even when you can't see him, he's always there. I giggle a little as I think about him lurking in the background, peering out from behind a bush or something.

"Hey," I say back with a grin, imagining his dark hair and eyes peeking over our backyard fence.

Good friends are like stars. I wonder if Jake thinks of us as good friends. I was so focused on not being teased about him that I pretty much ignored him all year. But here he is, still talking to me, still grinning at me, still caring if I'm okay. I used to think that I knew what a good friend was. But after this thing with Savannah, I'm not sure anymore.

"Warming up for my big debut," he says. He tosses the soccer ball in his hand over to me and I bounce it off my knee, down to my foot, and back up to my knee again. Jake looks impressed. "Not bad, Marathon Girl. Maybe you can be my assistant."

"Ha!" I say back. "Who's the assistant here?" I take the ball and show Jake a juggling trick my mom taught me. I flick the ball high up into the air with my toe, and then spin around and catch it on my thigh.

Jake laughs and bows down in front of me. "Master!"

I'm having so much fun with Jake that I forget how worried I was when I came in the door this morning. Maybe that's what a good friend is. Someone who helps you forget about the hard stuff. For a minute, anyway. As I'm thinking about not thinking about the hard stuff, out of the corner of my eye, I see Savannah walk in. Seeing her almost makes me lose my nerve, but then I picture myself as an alien fish, slowly descending into the sticky ick, and throw my shoulders back. I can do this. I will not be a lonely lungfish.

"Okay! It's a new day!" Jane gathers us together in a circle for what seems like is going to be a pep talk. I look over at Mr. Sharp and see that permascowl on his face, and wonder if this talk is more for him than it is for us. I look more closely and decide that I feel kinda bad for him. Poor guy seems to have been born with that look on his face. I wonder if he had any friends like stars when he was a kid like us.

"So today," Jane continues, "we are going to run through Kids Think! with Annie, as well as a few other segments we're considering adding in. Everyone, please welcome Jake Ramirez, who was not here with us on Tuesday, but is going to demonstrate some soccer moves for us today." We all clap for Jake who acts like he's embarrassed but I'm pretty sure is eating it up.

"Savannah," Mr. Sharp cuts in, "we have your script today. It's right here in my hand, and I'm not letting it out of my sight." He shakes the papers around in front of us. "We'll practice your introductions and transitions. Those might seem insignificant, but they're important to the overall flow of the show."

Raina hands Jake and me copies of the script as well. "Pay close attention. Follow along, because when she introduces you, you need to be on your mark and ready to go." She points out our marks, which are on opposite sides of the room.

"You've got this, Annie," Jake says to me as I walk over to my mark. My stomach twists a little as I think about what I'm about to do, and I suddenly realize that I am *not* worried about whether or not I'll get to be on *The Cat's Meow*. This thing that felt so important—that felt like everything to me—doesn't matter as much anymore. The only thing that matters to me in this moment is fixing my friendship with Savannah.

I echo Jake's words to myself and try to relax my tensed muscles. "You've got this, Annie."

Savannah goes to her mark with her script in hand. "We're going to start with Kids Think!" Mr. Sharp says. I make sure I'm in position. "Places, people! And . . . action!" I find my lines in the script I was handed.

"Welcome to today's edition of *The Cat's Meow*! I'm your host, Savannah Summerlyn." Savannah sounds exactly like she should. Very professional. My eyes jump down the page to the part where Savannah introduces me. It reads:

Here at The Cat's Meow we love it when kids use their noggins.

(Savannah taps side of head.)

That's why we will have a regular segment on our show called, Kids Think! Kids Think! is all about kids like you coming up with products that they think should exist. Kids Think! is the brainchild of the talented Annie Brown, who happens to be my very best friend. So buckle up and enjoy our very first segment of Kids Think!

But when Savannah reads the script in front of the camera, she doesn't read it exactly like that. She reads it word for word until she gets to the best friend part. She says, "Kids Think! is the brainchild of the talented Annie Brown." And she hesitates. It is ever so slight, but I definitely catch it. Then she continues, "So buckle up and enjoy our very first segment of Kids Think!" I can feel the heat climbing up my cheeks. Not quite Apple Anger, but maybe more of a Bewildered Blush. I look around, but Jane and Mr. Sharp don't seem to have noticed Savannah's revision of the script. The part where she *didn't* say we were best friends. Jake definitely noticed, because he's looking down at his script, and then I see his eyes wide looking at me. It's a sort of *What was that?* look, and I have to ignore it, because if I think about it too much then I might lose my nerve. I remember the word *pluck* that Dad taught me and think it's perfect for this moment, because I really, really need to be plucky. I don't even know if *plucky* is a real word, but to me it sounds like a combination of *brave* and *lucky*. And that's definitely what I want to be right now.

It's my turn. I breathe deeply and try to get the

Bewildered Blush to at least lighten up to a Pleasant Peach. I follow the script exactly: "Thanks, Savannah! I'm so glad to be here on *The Cat's Meow*! I hope you'll enjoy today's edition of Kids Think!"

"Great, great," Mr. Sharp says. "That's exactly the kind of tone we want. Did everyone get that? Okay, Annie. This is where you'll go into whatever commercial you have for us that week. If we decide to greenlight the segment then we'll have props for you to work with, but for now, let's just read through one, try to get a feel."

This is it. The moment I've been waiting for.

I look Savannah right in the eye and promise myself I won't look away from her until I'm done.

Have you bungled things with your bestie? Messed things up with your mate? want to settle things with your sidekick? Have we got the product for you! It's the:

FRIENDSHIP FIXER

Simply plug in the name of your friend and the mistake you made, and it produces that ace apology you've been looking for. Want to tell Savannah you wish you could take back what you wrote? Put your request in the FRIENDSHIP FIXER, and it will spit out that special sorry. Repair your relationship with no risk, thanks to our money-back guarantee!

Call or click now, and let the FRIENDSHIP FIXER help you make peace with your primo pal!

As I finish speaking, Savannah's face softens, and it reminds me of that day she moved in next door during my birthday party. Truth is, I wasn't so sure about having a kid I didn't know show up at my piñata. And when the first thing she did was bust right through Princess Pomeranian, I really wasn't sure. But as the candy flew through the air, Savannah didn't dive for it like the other kids. She hung back, not caring whether she got any candy or not. Which is super weird when you're talking about six-year-olds. Even though we had just met, she called out directions for me, to the spots where she saw the candy hiding. "There's one on the sidewalk! Hurry, Annie!" That's the thing about Savannah. She's always been happy to see me get the things I wanted. Whether it's cinnamon taffy or *The Cat's Meow*, she's always been my cheerleader. From the very first day we met. She really is *my* troubadour. And even though she has every right to be mad at me right now, I see her face and know that she is still cheering for me.

Savannah looks at the camera, and wraps it up. "And there you have it, another brilliant idea from Annie Brown, our Kids Think! correspondent and . . ." There's a very dramatic pause here, and I worry that Savannah has forgotten her line. But then I look down and see that she's gone off script once again. On the paper, there is no "and . . ." She smiles wide right at me, the biggest smile I've seen on her face in a long time, and finishes, ". . . my very best friend."

CHAPTER 26

"Cut!" Mr. Sharp calls out. "That's great. Good work, Savannah. You nailed it. Annie, please see Jane about your commercials—we need to make sure they are approved by production before we run them on air. That Friendship Fixer was not on my list." He looks over at me, then to Savannah, then back to me again and nods. "But it was a keeper."

A keeper? I guess Mr. Sharp is more like my dad than I thought. I imagine Mr. Sharp using the word *stinker* and have to hold in my giggles.

"And I'll need to consult with Ms. O'Malley, of course," he says, looking over at Jane, "but I like the direction Kids Think! is going."

Jane smiles at me and nods vigorously. "I agree. Congratulations, Annie!"

I can't believe it! I'm in! I look over at Savannah, who is literally jumping up and down for me. She even does one of her high kicks and waves her script around like a pom-pom. Jake is beaming at me, and waggles his eyebrows around like a total goofball. I realize that it's his turn now, and what I want to do is let him know that I'm cheering for him, too. My insides knot up as I see that he's all the way across the room, and everyone has quieted down in anticipation of the next segment. Which means that anything I say to him will be heard by absolutely everyone in this room, including Phoebe. The last two weeks flash through my mind and I think about how in the middle of all this drama, Jake has been the bright spot—just like a star. Jake has been a good friend to me. And I'm finally going to be a good friend back.

"Hey, Jake," I call out, not caring who hears me, "you've got this!" He smiles at me, and I smile back.

"Okay, Jake! You ready?" Jane calls Jake over to his mark. Savannah and Jake go back and forth on their script, and Jake expertly demonstrates how to do a toe flick. A toe flick sounds fancy but it's just a way to get the ball from the ground into the air with your feet. A much simpler way would be to pick it up, which is what I do most of the time when I start a trick. But trust me, you should never *ever* suggest picking the ball up to a soccer person. Most soccer people would love it if your hands disappeared altogether during a soccer game. WAIT. That's a really good idea!

Is soccer your favorite sport? Love the beautiful game, but hate how those pesky hands itch to touch the ball? Tired of hearing that referee whistle blow for a handball? Well, have we got the product for you!

Introducing

KICK KUFFS

Tie those hands behind you while
you play so they don't get in your way!
With KICK KUFFS handballs will be
a distant memory.

order an entire set in matching
team colors for only $19.95!

*Disclaimer: Not intended for goalkeeper use.

I lock my wrists behind my back and jog around a little, trying to get a feel for it. Hmm. Didn't think about needing your arms to run. A team with Kick Kuffs would end up being the slowest soccer team in history. This one might be a stinker.

"Annie, are you okay?" Phoebe shows up by my side, and once again she probably thinks I'm crazy-pants. I don't blame her, since I'm doing this funky Kick Kuffs demonstration mostly inside my head.

"Yeah," I say. "I'm working on a new product idea."

She points to Jake as he flicks the ball up with his toe and says, "Wouldn't it be easier to pick it up?"

My mouth drops open. If it were Savannah standing next to me, I'd say something like, "Right?" or "Totally!" or "I was thinking the same thing!" But it's Phoebe, and I'm not used to us agreeing on something. So I look at her and say nothing. Again, crazy-pants.

"That's why I like kickball," she continues. "You just kick it hard and run. Not a lot of extra rules." Phoebe. Kickball. Last time I thought about those two subjects together, I imagined myself launching Phoebe off of home plate for a game-winning grand slam. But today, something is different.

"You're really good at kickball," I say.

Phoebe tilts her head to the side and looks hard at me. She's definitely Perplexed Pink. "Thank you?" She says it like a question, like she's not sure if I'm being real with her. But I don't mean it in an ironic way at all.

"Annie," Phoebe says, "I really like the Friendship Fixer. I wish something like that actually existed."

"You do?" I say.

"Yeah, I could probably even use it right now," she continues. I raise my eyebrow at her, not sure what she means. "I wish I was as creative as you are. Savannah has been telling me about some of your other wrinventions, and they're really great. I especially like the cupcake shop you designed for your mom. I would go there!"

"Savannah told you about that?"

"Yeah, she didn't like it that I called your commercials silly. I'm sorry I said that. You and Savannah are just so lucky to have each other. I've never had a best friend."

"Never?" I ask. I can't believe it. Phoebe looks a little sad as she shakes her head, and I can't help but feel sorry for her. I think about Phoebe sinking down, down, down into the icky muck, and it doesn't give me the good feeling I thought it might. No one should have to be alone like that, not even Phoebe.

"Well, who knows?" I say. "Maybe this is the year you finally get one. Or two!" Phoebe gives me a surprised look, like I just told her the moon was made out of marshmallows. I kind of can't believe I said it, either, but after I do, I realize that I actually mean it. Uncle Walt would be proud.

We watch Jake as he finishes up. "This has been Mastering Moves with Jake Ramirez, the Finest Forward in Futbol!" He winks and points at the camera, making him look a little like a cheesy game show host.

But Jane loves it, because right after Mr. Sharp yells, "Cut!" she claps for Jake and says, "Perfect! Just perfect!"

I wave Jake over to us. "Way to go, Triple F!" I say. Jake looks at me, confused.

"Triple F?" he says.

"Finest Forward in Futbol!" I say

"I think we're both in, MG," he says, holding his hand up for a high five.

I glance over at Phoebe, who is still standing next to me, but then decide it doesn't matter. I high-five him back just as Savannah comes bounding over. She stands between us, with her left arm draped around Phoebe, and her right one around me. It's only a half hug, so I'll allow it.

"Oh, I almost forgot!" Phoebe says to me. "I saved these for you." She reaches down and digs around in her backpack.

"I tried to tell her cinnamon is your favorite," Savannah says. "But she insisted on saving these ones for you." I look down at the handful of candies Phoebe gave me and laugh. I definitely could get used to Phoebe.

They're orange. Every single one.

CHAPTER 27

"Savannah?" I knock on her bedroom door. Usually I bust right through it, but today feels different. She opens the door and waves me in. I sink down into the beanbag chair next to her dollhouse. There's still a hole in the roof.

"My mom thinks there is a way we can fix your dollhouse," I start. I want to talk to her more about *The Cat's Meow*, but for some reason it feels so much easier to talk about the dollhouse.

"It's okay," Savannah says. "Lynda said she'd take care of it." Our eyes meet and we both smile.

It's easy to be mad at someone when you aren't with them. You can sit in your bedroom and get madder and madder inside your mind. Like one of those cartoons where the guy's face turns bright red and steam comes out of his ears. You can make yourself feel like your head's going to explode and all the wrong things that were done to you are going to come pouring out like lava down the face of a volcano.

But just like you can sometimes remember belly flops differently to make yourself feel better, you can also sometimes remember things differently to make yourself feel worse. Which is definitely silly, because who wants to feel worse? But one day your almost-always best friend does something little, like eats your last cheese puff, and it's no big deal. But later, when you're alone, you're suddenly thinking about how she ate that last cheese puff, and how she certainly knew it was the last one, and how hungry you were, and how she snatched that cheese puff right out of your mouth anyway. And before you know it, the lava is pouring out, destroying every-thing in its path. Over a cheese puff. When you're not with someone, you can accidentally remember them like they're the villain instead of your friend.

But then you are with them and they say some-thing that makes you smile and you remember things the way they actually are instead of how you made them out to be in volcano-land.

"I'm sorry about *The Cat's Meow*," Savannah says. "I didn't mean to steal your audition. I just . . . I have something for you." She stretches out her arms in front of her. Perched in her palm is the glass quail. "I want you to have it."

"But, why?"

"You have more spirit than anyone I know," Savannah says.

I wonder if Savannah knows about the word *pluck*. I think back to just two weeks ago, when all I wanted in the world was to be able to say that this award was mine. So much has happened since then, and I surprise even myself when I say, "Thanks, but this award is yours. You earned it, and I'm proud of you."

From my back pocket I pull out a card. It has blue and yellow sparkly balloons on it, and in big red letters it says CELEBRATE! On the inside, I wrote:

Dear Savannah,
Congratulations on being the host of
The Cat's Meow!
From your almost-always best friend,
Annie

"Almost-always best friend?" Savannah asks.

"No one is perfect," I say. "That's what makes the world so interesting!"

"But we could try to be always-always best friends, couldn't we?" Savannah asks.

I think about it for a minute. Always-always best friends sounds pretty good to me. I take the card back and cross out the "almost-always best friends" part and replace it with the word *troubadour*.

"*Troubadour?*" Savannah asks. "Is that a word you wrinvented?"

Savannah laughs as I describe their outfits, but I think she gets the idea. I hold out my pinkie. She links hers to mine and we squeeze them tight.

"Troubadours?" I say.

Savannah agrees, "Troubadours!"

CHAPTER 28

"Fifteen minutes until lights out!" Dad's voice echoes down the hallway.

"I can't go to sleep! I'm full of inspiration! I have to write it down now!" I yell back. I'm working on my segment for next week's episode of *The Cat's Meow*—I need to run some more commercials by Jane tomorrow.

"You sure know how to melt the heart of a writer," Dad says, shaking his head as he walks through the bedroom door.

"You can't turn off inspiration, Dad."

"Don't I know it," he says, sitting down on the bed next to Evan. Evan is wearing his martian costume from Halloween, and reading a book about a robot that was sent into space. As soon as Dad sits down, Evan closes the book and climbs on Dad's back like a jungle gym

"Take me to your leader," Evan says in his best robot voice.

"Leader? Who called for a leader? Here I am!" Mom must have had a good day, because she comes in carrying a tray with apple cinnamon cupcakes and milk.

I scribble down one final thing and close my notebook. We eat our cupcakes while Dad tells us a story about a mouse on roller skates. It's a stinker, but we laugh anyway. After they tuck us in, Evan and I whisper in the dark, and I tell the mutant wrangler about the nickname I gave Jake, and how Phoebe wants me to come up with a nickname for her, too.

"What about me?" Evan asks. "What's my nickname?"

We toss around some ideas, and decide on "Bionic Boy" after Evan confesses to me that he's ready to move on from aliens to robots. He dozes off and his sweet little snore-sigh starts to lull me to sleep. Just as my eyes are getting too heavy to keep open, I have the best idea. A machine that generates nicknames! I pull out my flashlight and notebook from the bedside table and start writing.

Tired of generic, boring nicknames? Sick of sugary pet names like honey, sweetie, and cupcake? Well, have we got the product for you! The NICK-NAME NEGOTIATOR is a machine like no other! Just input all the things you love into our one-of-a-kind machine and we'll use our groundbreaking technology to formulate your perfect nickname! Listen to these testimonials from our satisfied customers:

"My whole life, I've wanted a nickname. My uncle, Burt Baxter of Burt Baxter Ford, used to call

me 'Angelcake' but now that I'm older I need some-thing cooler. I put all of my favorite things into the Nickname Negotiator and in seconds, it spit out the most excellent nickname. Now, all of my friends call me 'Pinky Pup' and I love it!"

I giggle to myself as I realize I've just cast Phoebe in another commercial. I decide to write in parts for Savannah and Jake, too.

"I already had one nickname I liked but the Nickname Negotiator has given me more options than I thought possible! Now I can be 'Savannah Songbird' when I feel like singing, or 'Duchess of Dance' when I feel like moving and shaking!"

It takes me a few minutes to come up with it, but it's perfect for Savannah. She'll love it. Last is Jake's, but his is easy. *"Chalk another one up for the Nickname Negotiator! It really hit the nail on the head when it came up with 'Smiley McSmilerton' for me. How did it know?"*

I laugh out loud at my own joke and then quickly

clamp my hand over my mouth so I don't wake Evan. I put the notebook away again and lie back down, thinking about what the Nickname Negotiator might come up with for me.

Triumphant Troubadour? Princess of Pluck? I think about "honeykin" and "Marathon Girl" and decide that maybe nicknames aren't so bad after all, especially when they come from people that care about you.

And as I drift off to sleep, thinking about wrinventions and robots, pink puppies and dancing songbirds, nicknames from dads and smiling boys, I decide that they're keepers. All of them.

ACKNOWLEDGMENTS

When I tell people that my high school mascot was a troubadour, I'm usually met with confusion. *What is a troubadour? Why would that be your school mascot?* While the role troubadours played in their era is somewhat difficult to explain, I've always imagined them as the ultimate encouragers, whose music and lyrics both uplift and challenge. I am blessed to have countless troubadours in my life, without whom this book would not exist. So this is my love song of gratefulness back to you—I promise not to sing it.

To my writerly friends, Dorina, Bethany, and Marcy. I love our years of laughing, sharing, and waiting together. Oh—and writing, too! And to Anne-

Marie and Gemma, who both gave transformative critiques of this story.

To Julie Matysik, who has cheered me on since day one, and placed this story in the hands of my fabulous editor, Adrienne Szpyrka. Thanks to Adrienne and Teresa Bonaddio and the whole team at Running Press Kids, for loving Annie and for asking all the right questions at the right times.

To agents extraordinaire, Laura Biagi and Jennifer Weltz. I am so happy to be a part of team JVNLA!

To my village at Jefferson Elementary School. Thank you for loving my kids and always being willing to lend a hand. My life doesn't work without you!

To my six siblings, who taught me early on that it was possible to find focus in the midst of chaos. And to my four amazing children, who reinforce that concept daily. To all of my family, near and far, I'm incredibly grateful for your support.

And to Rob, who, after twenty years together, still brings me cinnamon taffy because he knows it's my favorite. Thank you for being my always-always best friend.

ABOUT THE AUTHOR

AMY DIXON is the author of the picture books *Marathon Mouse, Sophie's Animal Parade,* and *Maurice the Unbeastly.* She writes from her home in Clovis, California, where she lives on a steady diet of popcorn and coffee. This is her debut middle grade novel.